I chase because you're mine.
I bite because you beg.

THE
HUNT

A FATE'S BITE NOVELLA

ELENA M. REYES

Summary

I chase because you're mine.
I bite because you beg.
And on All Hallows' Eve, your monster comes out to play.

No rules. No mercy. No limits.
Nothing stands between fate's bite and hunger, the need to mount and satisfy their females as they give in to the dirtiest of traditions— the hunt. It's predator versus prey under the full blood moon.

Claws. Fangs. Blood.

Theodore Astor stalks his witch-turned Vampire Queen, dragging his pretty girl into the shadows for a midnight feeding.

Xadiel Evergreen ruts his little moon, knotting and breeding his Luna.

Leonardo Moore binds his precious one with magic and satin—spanking his Fae Queen—before taking her over and over…

It's primal. It's filthy. It's fate.

Let the chase begin.

THE HUNT
(Fate's Bite Series)
Written By Elena M. Reyes
Copyright 2025 ©Elena M. Reyes

This book is a work of fiction. Names, characters, places, and incidents are either the products of the author's imagination or are used fictitiously. Any resemblance to actual events or locales or persons, living or dead, is entirely coincidental.

Cover Designer: EMR
Editor: Marti Lynch
Genre: Paranormal Romance/Suspense/Dark/Smut

Publication Date: October 31st, 2025

TRIGGER
WARNINGS

This book contains material that may be triggering for some readers.
It includes the following:

Violence & Death
Touch Her & Die
Explicit Sex
Blood Play
Werewolf (Monster)
Vampire (Feeding)
Spanking/Punishment
Explicit Language
Biting/Mating Mark
Some Primal Play
Obsessive MMC
Morally Grey
Knotting

This is for the willing PREY.
May your MONSTER always find you.
#bookboyfriends

Elena XoXo

Beware

Stay out of the shadows on All Hallows' Eve...
 A warning whispered by elders, taught from the cradle in fear and reverence.

You are never alone. Always being watched. And yet, it's changed over the decades.

Mortals think it's a game. A celebration that doesn't belong to them.

Lanterns, candies, and masks—laughter to hide the tremor in their own blood.

A warning they ignore. They do not see what waits beyond the glow of firelight.

Can't smell it. Cannot feel it.

But it is there...

Hungry. Watching. Waiting.

Because for the marked, those bound by fate, this night is a sacred rite. A claiming that thrums in their veins, and the impulse to claim is all-consuming.

Claws. Blood. Fangs.

Flesh pressed against flesh, woven bonds pounding as the world narrows down to the scent and taste of a mate...

Every touch and bite is a signed declaration.

Each gasp and shiver becomes an offer of submission.

Need. Devotion. Worship. *Mine.*

Under the blood-red moon, instincts rage unchecked, and love bends to hunger. Bodies writhe, slick with sweat and blood—trembling beneath a monster's touch as desires become feral. There's no pause, either.

Magic hums like a live wire as it wraps around limbs and throats, leaving sensitive flesh pulsing as the hunger to breed heightens.

Nothing fucking matters.

The hunt begins with a whisper of a scent; a pulse that cannot be ignored.

The monster is alive and breathing, its claws and teeth aching, and nothing will satisfy the thirst for blood until its mate is pinned and screaming.

No mercy. No rules. No shame.

This night is holy in its ferocity, sacred in its brutality, and dark in its insatiable calling for more...

Because this night is for the hunter and his wicked prey.

All others heed their warning growls.

"Run."

Pretty Girl

One
THEODORE

C an scent her arousal.

This decadent perfume is kissed by cherries and vanilla with the sensual tang of her blood. It calls to me with its heady and rich notes, the melody drawing a map only I can follow.

A private siren's song. Only mine.

It coils around me, sinking its claws into my restraint, and my fangs drop. They tear through my flesh as my nostrils flare and my tongue swipes across the sharp incisors—

She giggles.

Indulgently. In anticipation.

Because my pretty girl knows.

Tonight is a sacred night for our kind, a celebration for most, but for me, it's a sacred honor.

Every Hallows' Eve, I give in to nature's demand that I *hunt*.

A tradition I never paid attention to. Never heeded its call… until *her*.

My mate. My queen.

Closing my eyes, I inhale deeply while picking up the slightest noise. There's the chime of an old grandfather clock she loves and I hate, the raking of a branch across a window—my head shifts in the direction of the stairs where her delicate footfalls seem to be in a rush.

I'll give her efforts a passing grade, but we both know it's useless.

"Motherfucking adorable," I croon, counting slowly from one to thirty before opening my blood-red eyes again. I'm nothing if not generous. "I'm coming for you, pretty girl."

The corridors are silent except for the low hum of chandeliers, their gold filigree dripping shadows across black marble floors. My subjects have already fled the royal ground, heeding my warning. They know what tonight means. Know and accept that for her, I will kill.

I've done much worse over the last century without remorse or hesitation, and they expect nothing less from their king.

Gabriella Astor is in every stone of this castle, her scent embedded in the woven tapestries and linens—in me. She's mine to protect, to cherish, to ruin if I wish—she's my world.

Always has been. Always will be.

Licking my bottom lip, I catch traces of her wetness in the air surrounding me. The tethers of her magic and arousal lash across my senses as a snarl tears loose from my throat. The echoes of it vibrate against the wall like thunder rolling through a gothic cathedral, booming and ominous as I take my first step in her direction.

Because the beast in me wants to play.

Show her who she belongs to. Who's worthy of owning her.

"Run, little witch." As if she heard me, my pretty girl laughs and dances ahead, the sound high and wicked. The sound feeds me. Her scent also sharpens. It's sweeter, thicker, and intoxicating in a way nothing else will ever be. No blood or cunt will ever satisfy or soothe this demon.

Another five steps, and something flies by my shoulder, crashing into the dark walls behind me. On impact, it shatters into small crystal shards, pinging off skin it will never damage.

Bad girl baiting her mate.

Reckless little witch.

I picture the gleam in her eyes as she runs barefoot through my castle, wearing nothing but a thin satin slip the color of midnight. Dark. Soft. Barely there. The fabric shifts with her movements, accentuating every dip and curve—her perky breasts and soft thighs —that I'll mark with my bite before the sun greets the sky in a few short hours.

"I can scent your arousal, pretty girl," I call out, voice low and amused as the words slide along the walls until they reach her. And when they do, her soft gasp is my reward, a beautiful little tell she tries to smother and fails, forgetting that sound belongs to me.

Her moans. Her pleas. Her cries.

Every single one is mine.

My footsteps are slow at first, boots heavy against marble, and each one is deliberate as I move closer to the staircase landing. There, I stop. From the highest floor overlooking the elegant foyer, I find her...

Hair a blaze of red against gold and black décor.

Her back is to me, and her head is tilted to the side.

A slow shiver runs down her spine as lightning cracks outside the windows.

I smirk at the tiny beauty. Compared to me, she's a doll.

A very naughty one, as my nose twitches and eyes focus on a trail of sanguine beads stopping at her feet. There, they create a small pool; I notice a cut on her wrist where she's nicked herself on purpose.

And when she turns, looking at me from over her shoulder, I find my answer.

Challenge in her eyes. Lips stained red and curved up into an alluring smile.

A hybrid. Part witch. Part vampire.

The best of both worlds, and her small fangs slick with blood, is a challenge I accept.

"I love you, Gabriella." My voice is deep, the visceral manifestation of the demon she's taunted. "You are my world and the owner of this dead heart, pretty girl, but tonight…" I trail off, my chest vibrating with her purr as I remove my shirt and then pants, the tattered remains landing on the floor. I'm naked before her. Every inch of me is hard and throbbing. "Tonight, I will fuck you like my whore and bathe you in my come. I will feed from you, my mate. I will hurt you."

Her smile is as dangerous as she is. Red lips are lush. "I'm not afraid of you, Theodore. Do your worst."

"Good girl." My lips curve into a smug grin, but it drops a second later. My little prey has made a brave, yet very silly mistake. Eyes on mine, Gabriella lifts her wrist to her face and drags the bloodied mess down her cheek and the curve of her throat.

Over her pulse point.

The scent is powerful and rich. The literal definition of provocation.

"Are you okay, my king? Is there something you need?" she sing-songs, but I don't respond. Instead, I fight back the need to satiate this pulsing hunger. *Not yet.* Because if there's anything a monster enjoys more than his meal…it's the *chase*.

To stalk. To revel in the scent of fear.

For one hundred and twenty seconds, I just stand and watch her.

I catalog the changes in her breathing and the nervous twitch of her fingers. How her breathing accelerates and the smirk on those red-stained lips becomes a *pout*.

Plump fucking mouth.

"Run." One word. A promise and a threat.

And it has its desired effect. I'm not her mate and husband at the moment.

The door slams open, banging against the wall as my pretty girl sprints through the rain. There's a small, kittenish sound that leaves her as I count to ten. I let her put distance between us. Feel the thrum of her powers as her magic tries to weave false trails, yet the bond between us denies each one.

There isn't anywhere in this world my pretty girl could hide from me.

"Eight...nine...ten." Then I move as the world narrows down to her scent and the soft padding of her bare feet running across the wet field heading toward the forest. A rush of adrenaline pulses through me at that; I grip myself and give two slow pumps, savoring the moment. Pre-come beads and slips from the engorged head, the drops staining the marble floor as I slowly walk down each step.

A twist of my wrist and then the slide of my thumb heighten my need as I listen to her run.

I fuck my tight fist until reaching the final landing, and only then do I let go.

"Sanguis venari." *Blood hunt.*

Shadows bend around me as I run out the door, making it to the center of my guard's training field as she crosses into the crops of trees lining the forest. She hides within its darkness as the light mist turns into steady rain, small peaks of red catching my eye as the moon slips through the cropping. Gabriella is cunning and clever, I give her that. She's trying to mask herself again, but the decadent bloom of wetness pooling between her thighs is a beacon no amount of magic can hide.

You can't hide from me, pretty girl.

Once past the treeline, I study the ground for a second, my eyes taking in her footprints. They make no sense, and I smile. "Tricky little witch forgets who I am." They're almost in a circle, a few last-minute changes in the direction meant to confuse me, but there's one set that points straight ahead past *our* tree.

The only time I've lost to her in a skill challenge, we threw knives.

Fifty blades each, and the game? See how many we can embed without them falling out.

My mate cheated, but the blame is mine. The moment her small, delicate hand slid my zipper down and then slipped inside, gripping me, I fumbled the last throw. It's impossible for me to deny her anything, and more so when those soft lips moan for me.

She won: fifty knives to my forty-nine.

A chuckle escapes me as I pass by the embedded blade that sealed her win and tap the handle. "All's fair—"

"In love and war." Gabriella's voice comes from a few feet away, and my head snaps up, meeting her eyes. Her slip clings to her skin, soaked silk glinting like shadowed starlight. From her perky tits with hard nipples poking against material, to her wide hips and lithe legs, she's absolutely gorgeous. A temptation in female form. "Although I don't think you're hungry enough."

"Dangerous words, sweetheart."

"Or are they honest truths?" At her words, I let out a low hiss. In the past, that sound has made grown men whimper and plead, but my queen merely winks. Slowly. Deliberately. "Did I hit a nerve?"

My cock jerks at the provocation; I feel each bead of pre-come as it slips from the engorged head onto the forest floor below. The demon in me is marking his territory, but it's not enough.

Nothing but her pinned beneath me or sliding down my cock will ever satisfy this burning need...

Moreover, whatever my pretty girl sees on my face shakes her.

I feel her emotions as if they were my own.

There's excitement and a little fear, but more than anything it's...*greed.*

My pretty girl is just as obsessed with me as I am with her. Lovingly. Brutally.

It's always us. Only us.

Thunder cracks seconds after lightning strikes the open field behind us, but I pay it no mind.

Nothing and no one exists outside of this moment.

Another hiss slips past my fangs, and she answers with a kittenish sound dripping with approval—

"Catch me, Theo. I need you to break me." No sooner has the last word passed through her lips, my little mate turns and runs deeper into the woods. Drops of water run down her lithe body, the fabric stuck to her upper thighs, yet each pump of her legs moves the hem higher and higher until it's bunched just below the curve of her ass.

Round. Soft. *Mine.*

Her taunt is both cruel and brilliant. Fire lashes against my skin.

I don't say anything and watch her slowly get further away from me, a crime in itself, but I'm here to please, and if a bloody chase is what she wants, it's my honor to draw her blood. My lips curl into a grin that feels more like a snarl, my limbs vibrate with need, and the air seems still with anticipation.

Her magic. My power.

It's in the mist rising from the ground and the sway of tree limbs, but it's the heady scent of crimson cherries that drives me wild.

Delicious. So sweet. My cock throbs and jerks, the engorged head sensitive as I throw my head back while a guttural growl builds inside my chest. The sound rolls through the forest, echoing off the trees—her squeal comes a second later.

I take off toward the sound, tracking the trace of her scent and the faint shimmer of our bond. It's pulsing faintly in the dark, like tiny heartbeats of crimson light that fade as I approach.

A twig snaps a few feet from me, and my head snaps up.

"Gotcha."

"Not even close, King Astor."

"So bratty." I stalk forward, my bare feet silent against the cold ground. The tension coils tighter as she sprints toward another tree, hiding behind the thick trunk. Her head peeks out from around it a second later, gasping when her red eyes land on my cock. Immediately, her hands grip the bark, sharp nails digging in, and I use her distraction to my advantage.

On her next blink, I'm close enough to skim fingers across her plump mouth. Warm. Soft.

My pretty girl trembles, yet her expression is defiant. "You're making this too easy, my love. Lost your nerve?"

Her laughter rings out, faint and wicked. "Or maybe I'm letting you think you're winning."

"Then prove it."

"As you wish, My Lord." Stepping forward, Gabriella opens her mouth and pulls my fingers into her mouth, my nails drawing blood on her bottom lip. The sight is obscenely beautiful. My wife is my perfect match in every single way. "Now make it hurt."

She steps back, and my fingers drop, dragging down her chin and to the edge of her slip before she turns and runs away again. This time, though, my pretty girl doesn't look back.

Her low giggles fade into the rain, but the echo that answers is mine.

Low. Certain. Feral.

"Always, my pretty girl."

TWO
Gabriella

·······))) ● (((·······

Twenty Four Hours Ago…

The air inside my sanctum hums. It's thick with incense, candle smoke, and memories—knowledge passed down from generations and life experiences that carved different paths for the three Wiccan royals. I mated a vampire, my twin an alpha wolf, and our brother—the warlock king—he's tied to his beautiful fae in every way a man loves a woman.

We're happy. The universe blessed us, and yet no amount of time will ever fill the hole our parents' death left behind. There's no surpassing or healing that, but every small contact with their spirits temporarily soothes the dull ache.

Closing my eyes, I inhale deeply as my mother's favorite scent fills the space.

Patchouli and lavender; it wraps around me like her arms once did. A sense of warmth and comfort that takes me back to my youth and all the hours we spent learning from her. Lessons on growing herbs and creating healing tonics— learning to protect our lands with perimeter wards.

Baking and talking…daydreaming of the future.

Dozens of candles burn low, wax pooling over black glass holders. Their flames sway, bending toward the circle carved into the stone floor. Salt, ash, and two identical drops of blood bind the space: Isabella's and mine.

Across from me, Isa sits on a cushion, draped in white, her fingers poised above our father's grimoire. She's a bit distracted, but with Isa, it's best not to ask. Instead, you let her think and *see* without interruptions.

Three stones sit within the circle, while the altar is overflowing with offerings. There's an old record player crooning father's favorite songs, while a tray of my mother's beloved sweets sits beside large flower arrangements with her preferred blossoms.

The sudden breeze inside closed quarters makes me smile. I feel them.

They've never crossed. Our parents chose to remain in limbo, forever a part of our lives.

Isa looks up then, the glow from the candles making her look almost holy. She loves that. "Well, this is interesting."

"What is?" The lightest touch flutters through my hair, as if fingers were running through the strands, and it reminds me of Mom weaving daisies in my hair. Always so gentle, you barely felt it.

My sister doesn't answer. Instead, her eyes get glassy, gold bleeding through her blue irises, bright and burning, while her lips whisper something low. She also opens the grimoire, fingers running through pages until landing on a specific one.

The Blessing Of First Light

By first light and last breath, we welcome thee.

May your heart burn true, your blood run strong, and love guard your path until the stars forget our names.

The words shimmer faintly on the page, as if the ink remembers every time it's been read aloud.

"Isa…?"

"They're not alone tonight," Isabella says, voice low and full of emotion. She's not looking at me—her gaze is fixed somewhere beyond, straight through me—but whatever she sees makes her happy. Almost deliriously so. That same warmth floods through me, rippling across my skin until I swear I can feel our mother's joy. My father's pride. "Others are speaking."

The water inside the bowl begins to swirl while the stones within the circle begin to pulse. They represent their offspring; a trace of our magic is embedded in each one.

Isa jerks forward, gasping. "Oh Gods."

"What do you see, Sister?"

"Blood." Her voice trembles, bathed in excitement. I move closer and place my hand over hers on Dad's grimoire. I don't ask for her to elaborate. Instead, I give her a moment to blink a few times before her gaze settles on mine. The irises are gold before they flick back to her natural, baby blue. "New blood, Gabby. Three heartbeats beneath the next full moon, and they bring new gifts."

At once, the candles extinguish one by one, plunging us into darkness. Our parents' presence also vanishes, leaving my sanctum cold.

"But that's…" I stare at her, my chest tight. "And three?"

"Yes." Isabella nods, her smile radiant in the dark. "Three different cries."

"How soon? To whom?"

"A gift created beneath the next full moon and born to the three Wiccan royals…"

Present

THE GROUND SEEMS to tremble beneath my feet as Theo stalks behind me. He's letting me run ahead, amusing me by falling behind as I try to put some distance between us. I'm slipping between trees, ignoring the branches scratching my arms as my chest rises and falls with exhilaration.

I'm thrumming. A live wire of adrenaline and magic—part fear, part deep-seated craving.

For pain. For pleasure. For him.

Energy hums all around me—every heartbeat echoes in my ears as life breathes out its acknowledgement. I feel each pulse of the world around us: the life sleeping in the soil and the breath of dying leaves...

It *bows* to me.

Because I'm its balance. The one blessed by death.

Power flickers beneath my skin, at times too wild, and I draw it in, letting it roll through my veins as it sings. It's intoxicating. Sparks of life whisper to me, but one voice will forever rise above them all.

His. Always him.

Theodore's presence is impossible to ignore. It roars through the bond between us, dark and steady—relentless. A beacon in the chaos. He's my home.

And even when I run, my body still turns slightly toward him, like a compass seeking its north.

"Smug old bastard. All snarl, but no bite," I say, and it comes out like a whimper. He's so close...

"I'm going to make you pay for that remark, pretty girl. Mouth, cunt, and ass." The heat in his words cause me to shiver, almost stumble on a large root sticking out of the ground, and he takes advantage. Sharp claws graze my back, from lower back to the base of my neck, and the sting only serves to heighten my desires. A moment of pain with a promise of pleasure, and each wound blooms, the rich scent of copper headier.

Sanguine rivulets stain my clothes, sticking to my skin. The scratches aren't too deep, and I ignore the discomfort and pump my legs a little harder. He keeps my pace but lets me stay just out of reach, right before I slip inside a hollow tree with an exit on the other side. It's a straight-through shot, one he can easily counter by running ahead of me, but all I get is a sharp tug to my curls.

Hard. Fast. That jolt settles on my clit.

It causes my entire body to spasm, my hands shooting out to steady myself against the tree wall as my core clenches and my wetness coats my upper thighs. I'm swollen and sensitive. Throbbing, but the ruler of all vampires merely chuckles while leaning against the opening.

Crimson eyes watch me from beneath long lashes, his eyes hooded, while each muscle in his body contracts. Theodore is fighting back his instincts, and that won't do.

Turning, I fully face him while gripping the bottom edge of my slip and pulling the ruined garment over my head. I'm bare beneath. Wet, bleeding, and at his mercy—his answering snarl sends a shiver through me.

He takes a menacing step toward me, dick hard and pointing upward toward his stomach, and I watch in delight as Theo grips himself and strokes once, then two more times. He keeps his hold tight as he takes me in, and the way his gaze roams me is feral. Unhinged.

"Gabriella." My name on his tongue is sinful, a reverent caress across our bond.

"I live for you, my king." The wound on my wrist has begun to heal; I lift my arm and place the ravaged skin against my fangs. There's a faint trace of red on my teeth, but to make my monster snap, I will paint the world red.

Moreover, I am his world. Always will be, just as he is mine.

Sinking my incisors deep, I tear through my flesh until there's a constant drip. Red and sweet—a buffet laid out in front of a vampire who feeds solely on me. He's never taken a feeder or demanded I let him hunt; he lives to worship me while only taking what's necessary.

I want more. For him to be selfish for once.

As a turned vampire, I've never lost the side of me that's a witch.

My heart beats.

My body can digest human food.

My body naturally produces the one thing my mate needs.

Rich crimson that I hold above my naked body, watching in pure delight as his facial features tighten further, the hungry beast within him rising to the surface and growling his demands. His nails grow sharper, his fangs drop lower, and I can't help but clench my thighs when his cock jerks in his tight hold.

When his abs contract and every sinuous muscle thickens, Theo grips the tree's trunk with his unoccupied hand, nails digging in deep. The wood cracks while I let the blood drip. It runs down my body in streaks, from my breasts down my stomach until sliding down my mound. I feel each stream, but it's his heated gaze that makes me moan.

One second, he's across from me, and the next, Theodore has one arm wrapped around my waist while the other brings my wound to his lips. He kisses the cut. Once, twice…five times before licking across the wound. His groan is deep; it builds in his chest as my taste spreads across his senses.

I feel it in our bond.

He's pleased with himself as his saliva heals the torn flesh. "Only I hurt you."

Then he strikes. His head shifts, and his fangs embed themselves in my neck. Pain burst through me like a fiery lash, but then it morphs into unadulterated pleasure. It takes hold of me, spiking as Theodore lifts me and positions me just above his cock.

A single graze of the engorged, slick head, and I tremble. The orgasm slams into me, my juices making a mess of him as I open my mouth on a silent scream. He prolongs it, too.

He rocks his hips slowly through my sensitive labia and over my clit; I'm unable to fully catch my breath as another pulse of pleasure rocks me. Theo drinks from me in deep pulls, the sensation tickling a little, like an electrical pulse beneath my skin. The longer it goes on, the more it changes—turning heavy and warm, spreading through every nerve until I feel weightless in his hold.

My pulse slows, sinking with his rhythm, each swallow a heartbeat shared between us.

It's erotic. Raw. *Beautiful.*

The world's edges blur as the trees, night, and even the pain melt into a deep, satisfying thrum. His mouth moves more slowly now, reverent, sealing each breath with a low sound that vibrates in his chest. My king is purring for me, grounding and dizzying, the perfect blend of surrender and trust.

I am his. He is mine.

Seconds later, he lifts his head, lips glistening crimson, and his eyes…

Gods, he's beautiful. They're the brightest red, full of love and lust, yet the tenderness is there as he takes me in.

I'm a mess and pliant in his arms.

"You're so fucking beautiful, pretty girl."

"Theo, I—"

My mate cuts me off with a single, earth-shattering kiss. His mouth crashes onto mine, hard and claiming, leaving no room for a single thought. Sharp teeth clash, his hand gripping the back of my neck now to hold me still. It stings, but Gods help me, the taste of us is exquisite.

I can't tell where he starts and I end, and just as my hands finally function enough to grip his arms, I'm set down and he takes several steps back. I'm also not given a chance to ask him *why,* either.

Theodore turns, giving me his back, and begins to count. From one to seventeen, and then pauses, his head tilting as if listening for something. For a few seconds, neither of us moves, and then he snaps his fingers once, the same way he does right before giving out orders.

His aura fills the space, dark and dangerous. The temperature around us drops, the vampiric lands bracing for the wrath of its ruler, and gone is my mate, leaving a cold and deadly killer in its place.

A protective male.

"We're not alone, pretty girl. Come to me."

Three
THEODORE

·····•)❭❭●❨❨(•·····

Two heartbeats.

One steady and fast—panic and adrenaline pumping through veins that reek of alcohol. The other, though…it's slower. Labored. A dying rhythm.

Every movement cuts through the stillness. From the snap of twigs and mud sucking at rubber soles to the desperate shuffle of prey that doesn't realize it's already cornered.

They reek of cheap spirits and grime, drunken fools, but beneath the repulsive stench, there's more. A scent hits the back of my throat then, thick and cloying, with an abrasive undertone of sulfur that makes my mate grimace as her hand slips into mine.

I yank her to me before wrapping a hand around her waist, gripping tight. The one holding her hand now cradles the back of her neck, and I press her sweet face against my chest. She breathes me in a few times, her petite frame relaxing while her small teeth nip my skin more than once.

Naughty little thing. So playful.

The intruders move closer—heavy footsteps. They shouldn't be here.

My lands are protected, wards placed by Gabriella herself...especially for tonight. They're meant to keep the predators in and the living out, and yet these men have interrupted my private time with my queen. A fault of my own, one I'll remedy soon—the protection recognizes power, not intent—and these two reek of flesh and greed.

Stupid, weak humans.

"You think they're still chasing us?" a gruff, older voice asks. Beneath the tone, there's pain. A lot of it. "We've been running from the police for days now."

"Just a little further up." This man is definitely younger. Impatient. Annoyed. "The stupid witch said to follow the underground tunnels—"

I stop listening then. Completely unnecessary when the criminal mastermind is currently giggling in my arms, shoulders shaking, while the bond between us floods with amusement.

At the sound, the men pause, their acrid scents now tinged with want.

Curiosity. Fear. *Impatience.*

"Did you hear that, Jay?"

"I did, Son. A cute, girlish laugh." A groan leaves his lips, but that soon turns to coughs. "It's been a while since we've shared something tight and soft."

"That fucking witch interrupted our time with the blonde in the alleyway," the younger spits. His anger ripples from him, but beneath the false bravado, he's scared. On edge. I like it. "The redheaded cunt better be right about the gold and healing amulet. I won't help you again after this, *Father.*"

They're not far from us, picking up the pace while the sick one of the two struggles a bit. He stumbles, a few curses escaping, while I tug my pretty girl's hair back and force her red eyes up to mine.

Why Gabriella sent them here doesn't matter to me. They're dead men walking either way.

"You'll pay for this interruption, my love."

"Do your worst, Mr. Astor."

"As you wish." I slam my mouth down to hers, taking it in a quick and brutal kiss before flipping her around. Her back is to my chest, my arm tight across her midsection, before I move.

The air cracks as I leap, landing silently on a branch high above the forest floor. The wood bows, but doesn't break. It holds my weight, but the height doesn't hide her scream as I impale her on my shaft.

I'm buried to the hilt in one brutal stroke, her sweet little cunt stretching to accommodate me, and I revel in the way she clenches— her body giving in to the pleasure and pain only her mate could gift her. I don't stop either; I fuck her with relentless strokes. Suspended in the air, she's leaning on me and under my control.

I maneuver her to my liking. Hold her close, my unoccupied hand wrapping around her throat as I pump my hips at a rapid pace. There's no time to plead, much less hold back her screams, and the men run toward us now.

They ignore every warning. The air is filled with their groans and my wife's pleasure.

"Theo, I'm so close. Please don't stop."

"Come for me, Queen Astor. Bathe your king." The branch trembles, a few leaves falling seconds before the two intruders break through the trees. From our position, I see their heads turning left and right, their body language anxious, while my mate tightens. She's strung tight, breath shuddering, and every tremor runs through me before settling on my balls.

My cock drips pre-come against her walls, my fangs against her skin. This time, I bite down on her shoulder—she screams, loud and wanton. I tighten my grip on her neck. Own her.

Gabriella's caught between my hand and the night while the men below turn rabid. They're arguing, pushing each other, and trying to find the source, but come up empty over and over again. The younger looks up, but is distracted by the sudden rustling of a bush where a rabbit is trying to hide.

Fucking idiot.

"Theo, please," she whimpers. I can feel every tremor that rips through her, love the way her heady scent curls around us, and each pulse makes her tighter around me.

Her breath catches, and my control breaks.

The next snap of my hips is meant to hurt, and it's in that pain that my pretty girl comes for me. It crashes into her, each wave of pleasure ripping her apart until what's left in my grip is pliant and soft. So fucking sweet.

And it's only when the last tremor rocks her and she sags against me that I drop behind the men. If they notice me or not, it makes no difference. Their end won't change.

Before the first head turns, I punch through the younger man's back, tearing his heart out. His father sees my hand, takes note of the bloody organ held by my fingers, and meets the same fate before he can scream. Both bodies land with a dull thud, gaping holes in their chests and the useless muscles still twitching beside their bodies.

My pretty girl watches but remains silent, her pussy clenching and gyrating every few seconds as a recompense. It isn't enough. Not when this interruption is of her making, noble act or not.

I could've jailed them days ago and killed them after, but she wanted this. Chose this.

With that thought, I snarl and toss her into the air, turning her upside down in my grip. She squeals, blood spiking with adrenaline, then lust as her mouth hovers close to my cock.

I haven't come yet, and I won't, but that doesn't mean I'm not due a prize.

Another little shift, and my cock sits against her lips in this position. Her pussy is in plain view—spread as I take hold of her hips and begin walking back toward our castle. Stroll leisurely. No rush.

She's pink and soft, so fucking wet, and I watch how her juices flow from that tiny, clenching hole. It pools at her entrance. This position doesn't leave room for her wetness to drip, and I stop just long enough to lift her to my lips and run the flat of my tongue from her ass to clit, then place her back into position.

Her rough exhale against my engorged head feels good, but when she opens her mouth, tongue sliding…

"That's it, baby. Fuck, you're my good girl." At my praise, Gabriella whimpers, bobbing her head faster. She takes me from tip to base, using her throat as a cock sleeve a few times before pulling back so just the head sits on her tongue.

She flicks it. Sucks it. That sinful, pouty mouth worships me.

"Suck," I command, letting go of her right hip so I can smack her pussy with three fingers. I catch her bundle of nerves and slick lips hard enough to sting, and she tenses. Whimpers for me. Her slick juices splatter my chest. "I want to fuck that pretty mouth, Mrs. Astor."

"Please, Theo…" a cry this time, my direct slap to her cunt shaking her "…use me."

"Then open. Open and hold still." My mate does as I ask, lips wide with my swollen tip at the opening. Soft. Wet. Heat. "*Motherfucking* perfection."

It's a hiss. I thrust deep and fast, sliding down her throat until her lips meet the base. She swallows a few times, hollowing her cheeks as I continue to walk. Every few steps is a snap of my hips, enjoying her lack of a gag reflex as her throat muscles work me.

I'm not gentle. This isn't meant to be sweet.

I don't pause or slow down until we're inside our home and walking into the throne room.

Only then do I release my mate, pulling out from her swollen mouth. She complains, the sounds full of annoyance, but I ignore her.

Once she's on her feet and stable, I walk to the dais and sit on my throne.

Gabriella narrows her eyes; they're full of fire and demand an explanation. But I'm not the one who interrupted our playtime.

This is her game now, but the reward remains mine.

Come to me, pretty girl.

A few minutes of silence follow, but she cracks first. Her hips sway seductively as she walks across the room to stand below me, as if on trial. She's filthy, wet—dried blood decorates her body.

My feral little witch is perfection, but tonight I'm her judge and jury. Disciplinarian, too.

"I wasn't done, Theo."

"Is that so?" It's hard, but I bite back my smirk. "I thought you were."

Pretty girl bristles, and her eyes, which had softened into their natural green shade, flash red. *She's adorable when mad.* "Your orgasm is mine. Each drop of come belongs to me."

"Earn it."

"W-what?" Confused. Insulted. *Fuck, I love her.*

"You heard me, pretty girl." My cock bobs, a mix of spit and pearl-like beads of fluid leaving a mark on my abdomen. I don't touch myself, but her gaze feels like a caress. "The only way you'll get my come tonight is to earn it."

"Theo, I—"

"Not another word, love. Mount your king."

Gabriella sees this for what it is, walks up the two steps, and turns, giving me her back. She doesn't say anything. Instead, she bends forward and spreads her cheeks so I have the perfect view of her holes. They clench, and I slap her left asscheek, then the right one in approval.

With my other hand, I stroke myself slowly.

Let her tease, but my patience can only run for so long.

"Enough, Gabriella." Gripping my cock tight, I watch her sway her hips seductively as she takes her place between my parted thighs. She moves her ass, bouncing lightly to make the flesh jiggle before slipping a hand between her thighs and dipping a few fingers inside. In and out, she pumps them a few times, her slick juices running down her hand and onto the floor below, but it's the kittenish moan that has me grabbing those hips and lifting her above my cock. "Ride. Me."

Immediately, her fingers slip out as she moves to grip my arms. "I decide how I'll make you come. I'm in charge—"

Her words become a piercing cry as I slam her down on my cock.

It both angers and thrills her, and I'm taught a valuable lesson when she reaches down between us and squeezes my balls. With her back to my front in reverse cowgirl, I'm giving her the luxury of setting the pace, and after a few sharp tugs that send a wave of pleasurable pain through me, my pretty girl rides me fast and hard.

There's no testing the depth or building up slowly; Gabriella *fucks me* like the queen she is.

My girl leans forward and bounces, her hands using my knees as leverage, but it's not enough. We both know what she needs, but I indulge her nonetheless. Let her set the pace and chase the orgasm that's just out of reach, until her frustrated cries rend the throne room.

"Please, Theo. I can't..." she trails off, not stopping her gyrations, but the frustration mounts.

I nip her back with my fangs. "What do you need? Tell me."

"You." This time, it's a sob as I push the hand she's tried to slip between her thighs away. "Please fuck me."

"And the next time you want to kill someone, you won't sneak them onto our lands?"

"No." She sags against me, lying back, which changes the angle. Makes her tighter. "I'll be upfront and ask for help."

"We both know you could've killed them yourself. Why bring them here?"

At my question, she stops moving. Just stills while I'm buried deep, and she exhales roughly. "Because I wanted to be fucked by the monster you keep hidden."

"Now you've earned my come." No sooner has the last word passed my lips than my fangs are embedded deep into her neck. Sweet, rich blood fills my senses while my fingers are on her clit, rubbing tight circles on the bundle of nerves, and my hips piston from below. I drink from her, thrusting deep and fast while my good little witch takes the abuse.

And yet, she doesn't try to pull away. Instead, she angles her head and whimpers *more*.

Moreover, I oblige. I pound her cunt without mercy, taking deep pulls from her veins until her eyes roll back and the first rush of her orgasm coats my cock. Her thighs tremble, her walls pulsing—I retract my fangs and grip her neck, turning her face toward mine.

I find a blissed-out vampire witch, her expression soft yet still needy. "Kiss me, My king."

My mouth lowers to hers, slow and sweet, a complete contrast to the way I'm taking her pussy. Thrusting hard and fast, I'm hitting the spot that makes her weak while she cries into my mouth. Each pulse, each rush of wetness making a mess of us pulls me closer to the edge, but it's her low *I love you* that milks the come from me.

Rope after rope of spend fills her pussy to the brim and then overflows, staining the seat below us. Not that I give a single fuck. Every inch of the grand room smells like us, and my chest swells with pride at the satisfied grin on my pretty girl's lips.

Now she's happy.

"Thank you."

"And I love you." With her nestled against me, I lazily continue to pump into my wife. Time ceases to exist outside these walls; I'm held captive by the feel of occasional tremors running through her. She rests while I revel in her softness…

Love. Happiness. *Excitement.*

The last one is a surprise, but the bond tugs with the command for another round. Her eyes flash open, and I know that whatever it is, I won't say no.

"This time, I want you to bend me over in an alley like a whore and…"

Little Moon

FOUR
Isabella

·······•••))) ● (((••······

One Hour Before…

The cold bites like it knows my name.

It slips beneath my fur-lined cloak, sharp and alive, stirring the power coiled under my skin. The Alaskan wilderness is brutal this time of year, and yet I revel in its old magic. Like an old friend who's always watching, recognizing that I'm protected by its master, it bends to my will.

I'm a witch: protected by Gaia and cherished by the king of all wolves.

A luna: a source of comfort and guidance to our pack.

A mother: I'm raising an alpha born to one day command the gods and wolves alike.

Fair. Noble. Protective.

Three cries beneath the next full moon…

The trees know why I'm here. So do the Gods.

Born to three Wiccan royals.

We are to be blessed once more.

Gabriella's words echo in my ear then, pulling a smile from me. She'd looked at me with mischievous eyes, yet her expression was serious.

A challenge.

Run wild, my sister. Make him earn what's already his.

So I do.

Snow crunches beneath my boots as I move deeper into the pines, my breath a soft cloud of frozen air. The northern lights ripple above me in streaks of green and violet, the sky thrumming with the same energy vibrating beneath my skin.

Beautiful. Untamed. Dangerous.

Just like him. My male.

Xadiel thinks I'm still near the nest he's built for me, a dome made of glass with an open floor plan. It's where we come to isolate during my heats and his ruts, days on end where I'm ridden fast and hard and left a dripping mess stretched by his knot and full of come.

"Goddess, I need him," I whisper low, keeping myself beneath the rustling wind and thick, lush greenery. To him, I'm arranging my nest, but he forgets I bite back. I might not be a full wolf, but his mate mark and seed have given me certain *advantages*.

Claws. Teeth. Slick.

I was created to fit my seven-foot wolf like a glove.

Tight. Unbreakable. Strong.

He is my ruin. I am his fate.

Pausing beside a fallen birch, my gloved fingers brush across the rough bark as I crouch. My small claws extend then, pushing through the tips, slicing the fabric with ease as the air suddenly thickens. A shiver runs down my spine—half magic, half instinct—as I carve a circle into the tree.

"Mother Gaia, wake his beast," I whisper, pulling a small sash from the pocket of my dress. It's a mixture of salt and ash, and I sprinkle a few pinches over the marking. "Let the wolf inside tear free and hunt me with holy hunger."

The words are a prayer and command—a plea to unleash the monster I love. The fallen snow around the circle moves, subtle light pulsing faintly beneath the surface as energy builds. I feel the answer slice through our bond.

The spell doesn't just stir *him*; it stirs the bond between us— stretching, tightening, and burning. His howl in the distance is raw and powerful. A calling to his female, and my lips curve in satisfaction.

The spell hums again, and my vision ripples. Flashes of a vision flood my mind.

Xadiel's silhouette is framed by shadow and the aurora's light, a growl rumbling in his chest.

His breath on my throat.

The snap of bone and then pleasure tangle so tightly it's impossible to tell where one ends and the other begins.

And beneath it all—hunger. Thick and consuming. His *rut*.

My pulse stutters, magic burning through me as the image sharpens. His eyes are pitch black with just a golden ring around the iris, the beast inside clawing to the surface. It's not a warning, but a promise.

Magic and impulse collide.

The sight hits like lightning, fast and turbulent, then it vanishes, leaving behind a delicious ache in its wake. It's intoxicating, alive, and humming with an invitation to welcome and accept our fate.

I smile. "Tonight, he hunts for me."

Reaching into my pocket, I pull out a parchment I'd prepared earlier. Old and wrinkled, the paper reminds me of the ones my parents used over a century ago, while the ink carries a woodsy and mint note—same as him.

My pulse quickens as the scent settles over me, my adrenaline kicking in as I begin to write. The words flow in a rhythm older than my ancestors.

To my king of fangs and moonlight,
If you wish to claim your witch, seek the hollow
where the wind hums low and history remembers your
name. There I'll wait for you...
Desire on my lips and promise of sin beneath my
cloak.
Find me before dawn,
Little Moon

The words shimmer faintly, the tethers of my magic signing my oath while my now bloodied thumb seals it. Crimson magic binds my promise, the bite mark on my thumb barely visible as I place the note down for him to find.

But I'm not done.

I'm not making this easy for him.

I whisper an older spell, one passed down from generation to generation by the oracles of my coven. It's a mirage. A veil of illusion. The snow around me glows then stills, and the scent I'll leave behind remains thick in the air—my warmth and heartbeat stitched into the parchment.

To my male, it will feel as though I'm here. Waiting. Watching.

"I saw this, my love." Tapping the paper a final time, I stand with a smile. "The moment you find this note, breathe me in...the *hunt* begins."

Pulling the hood of my cloak over my head, I walk into the trees and disappear while humming a low tune. It won't take me long to reach my destination, but I plan to confuse him along the way.

I'll hide. He'll seek.

But more importantly, Xadiel will come for me with the hunger of a god reborn.

Five
XADIEL

"Where are you, Little Moon?" The question rasps out of me, low and rough as I leave her nest. It's snowing out, the late evening quickly turning dark, and my female is nowhere to be seen.

I don't like it, and neither does my wolf.

His senses are sharp, more alert than usual—demanding that I find her. It's there in his constant, low growl, the sound a warning but not from anger...

No. This is pure, unadulterated need.

The kind that burns through reason until instinct is all I have left.

Patting my chest, I try to soothe him, but the animal's claws rake my insides. His impatience, the driving force to find Isabella, becomes my sole reason to exist.

Mine.

Closing my eyes, I breathe in deep, searching for her scent...

Jasmines. Soft, dangerous, and sweet enough to drown in. It's surrounded by a trace of my scent, twisting into something uniquely ours.

Then, there's her magic.

It hums in the air. Its tethers like woven silk tugging me in her direction, pulsing yet delicate.

Always toward home. Because that's what she is.

My home. My life. My love.

"She was here," I say, jaw tight. I can still feel the echo of her heartbeat through our bond—the tug at my chest forcing me to walk away from the private nest I'd built for her in the Alaskan wilderness.

I'm following a map no one can see, but I know like the back of my hand. My mark on her throat and the traces of her scent let me find her anywhere, even if she cloaks herself with spells.

Because that's what this is.

She can't hide from me.

Not when I've been an excellent student.

"My female," I mutter, exhaling steam into the cold. "You're playing a dangerous game."

The air crackles then, and the moon rises high. It's All Hallows' Eve, a night where the veil thins and magic runs wild—my instincts sharpen to match it. Every year, we steal away from the world to feed this obsession that burns and thrives between us.

No crown. No pack. Just *us*.

These woods are empty. Our pack has left the area to hunt or has gone home to England so that their royal pair can have some privacy.

They know the law. Know my wrath.

I'm a fair alpha, but anyone—outside of a lost pup—who trespasses on our night will be dealt a swift death. That is the punishment, and it fits the crime. I do not share my female, and tonight, she will run wild and free as I chase, then mount my prize.

Except—she seems to be hiding from me.

I should be angry about this. I should be running, chasing her in wolf form. But instead, heat curls low in my gut.

She's made this into a sexy game of hide and seek.

A grin splits my mouth, sharp and hungry. I can feel the pull of her spell somewhere north, like a faint, teasing brush of her fingers over my senses.

You started this feral game, my love.

I start moving. The bond tightens as I do, drawing me forward through the snow, each breath filling me with more of her scent. Stronger. Sharper.

Excitement coils beneath my ribs, my cock straining against my trousers. The engorged head throbs, and beads of my seed pool, then slide down the shaft.

My knot also swells.

It's been sensitive all day, the skin tight, and each thought of her makes it harder to focus on anything but locking myself inside of her warm, wet cunt.

"I'm coming for you."

THE TREES CLOSE AROUND ME, heavy with snow. Every crunch beneath my boots is swallowed by the hush of winter. The world narrows down to impulses—the smell, sound, and the faint rhythm of her heartbeat echoing through the tethers that bind us.

Jasmine again, but stronger. And under that, I smell her blood.

Not enough to harm, just a drop offered in spell-work—the taste a ghost across my senses, lighting a spark through my veins. I don't know how long I trek through the woods, but I'm drawn to a fallen log with a note on top. It's folded neatly, edges rusted with frost.

Her aura surrounds it—me—here, a soft and warm tether trapped in paper.

Nothing else. No illusion.

Just her essence is a signature.

I reach for it carefully, my fingers brushing the edge when a jolt of power lashes through me. My eyes flash bright, then darken, the irises black as my wolf rises. He's pacing, pushing me to find his mate before I lose all rationality.

Already, I can feel the change.

It starts deep, an ache under my skin that turns molten in a single breath. My pulse hammers, heat flooding through me until the cold can't touch me, and every inch of me throbs for her. My vision sharpens as the bond pulls taut, and her scent is all I can see and understand.

Baser needs. Animalistic focus.

Nothing exists outside of her touch, her kisses—the way her cunt tightens right before my knot locks us together. I will not stop, either. Wolf and man have one singular focus, and that's to breed their female.

Shaking my head, I clear out the beginning rut-fog and take in her handwriting. It's elegant and clean—every word deliberate and utterly her.

To my king of fangs and moonlight...

I read the rest, jaw clenching while my upper lip curls into a snarl —my fangs drop, breaking through the gums almost violently. Each line is a touch I can't feel, a kiss I'm being denied. My mate is daring me to find her. Challenging her wolf to take the bait.

"Sneaky little witch," I growl, though the words taste like worship. Yet worse than the taunt is the lingering magic stroking the thick imprint of my cock over my trousers. It's slow, almost a bloody caress, and the rut answers before I can fight back the change.

Heat crashes through me, blood roaring as my muscles contract painfully, hunger tearing at the seams of my restraint.

My beast rises.

Claws break through my skin, blood dripping from each black-tipped talon as power threads through every place on my body she's ever kissed or bitten. Where she's marked me, irrevocably owning the man who lives to worship his female.

Dropping to one knee, my fingers dig into the snow as steam curls around me.

The world blurs in and out of focus as the fever takes hold. Winter presses in—pine, snow, and silence fight to control my senses —yet my focus is locked on her.

Jasmine. Always jasmine.

I bury the note beneath the wet ground, claws slicing through mud and frost, sealing her words away before the scent drives me mad. Lifting my head, I draw in a lungful of cold air. Her trail is faint but constant, a thread of warmth woven through the cold.

The howl tears from me before I can bite it back. It's raw, jagged, and full of need. The bond snaps in answer, hard enough to steal my breath as it yanks me forward a step at a time.

I have no control. It demands I move, hunt, and *find*.

My clothes tear, seams giving way to muscle and fur. Claws rip through the soles of my boots, my feet sinking into the snow as the mid-shift claims me. I am neither man nor beast—something in between and built to destroy. I'm seven feet of hunger and purpose, the blood throbbing in my veins calling her name.

She's moving fast. Too fast.

The forest blurs around me as I run, white clouds exploding under each stride. The northern lights bleed across the canopy, guiding me toward the place her riddle promised. My breath comes rough, steaming in the frigid air. Every inhale brings another lie meant to confuse me. The taste of her arousal bleeds into her sultry perfume; the mix is heady, and I grip myself with clawed hands.

With every ten steps, I stroke myself down and then up. I'm a monster. Feral and brutal. And yet, the only part of me that will hurt her is swollen, and the skin is taut, leaving behind a trail of pre-come on the white forest floor.

I bare my teeth, licking a fang. ***Run and hide, Little Moon. Make me earn you.***

The mindlink between us remains silent, but I know she heard. It's there in the love filtering through from her end, the small whine she can't control after a few minutes. No words, but that sound is enough to set my pulse ablaze.

Moreover, I fuck my hand as I replay that sound over and over. It's my preferred soundtrack as I head deeper into the Alaskan wilderness, where very few wander. Her clue was direct. I know the place well, but the thought of her out here alone doesn't sit well with me.

Isabella should be in her nest, cozy and warm and spread out for me like the gift she is.

My steps pick up their pace to match hers, heading in the same direction while ignoring the few fake trails that carry her essence. Meant to trick and deprive, but both man and beast cannot be deterred.

I run. The forest blurs past me, rushes of shadow and white as my strides shred the distance. Her trail veers through trees, weaving between birch and pine, dipping into hollowed earth and curling back again. Then, there's the illusions that flicker, movement to my left one second, then the right, and it's always flowy strands of red hair that curl at the ends.

The sight is accompanied by her giggle. Bright. Warm. Playful. A complete contrast to the wind cutting across my face, sharp as a blade, the sting pushing me harder. Faster.

Find me, my wolf.

Her words through the mindlink catch me off guard, my body tensing, but I'm able to jump over the large root sticking up from the ground. My wolf snarls at her through our connection, not that it does much as she snorts.

I'm coming for you, Isabella. This is your only warning.

Before she can reply, I cut the connection and turn left, where an old bridge connects to a denser crop of trees leading to a ravine. But more importantly, it's where I find a small piece of white fabric I'd recognize anywhere. Soft satin stitched at the hem with our initials.

X. ♥ I.

I slow as I reach it, picking it up and bringing it to my nose.

It's her. Potent and decadent. *Mine.*

Movement ahead catches my attention, but I pretend otherwise. Ignoring my mate, I run the piece of fabric across my swollen head, swiping the pearl-like beads there, marking the satin.

I'm not going to bring it with me, but bend and place it where she left it, her scent and mine combined, as it always should be. She's watching this, the small mewl she makes, proof of her inability to stay away either.

I also catch her sharp intake of breath. Scenting me. Noting the change.

Isabella is where the ridge breaks and the forest dips into shadow, just as the riddle stated. And when I cross, my clawed feet firmly planted not far from her hiding spot, my mate steps out. Gone is her dress; she's wearing nothing but her favorite cloak over her bare skin. Soft, creamy flesh is on display while the ravine walls are slick with ice and moss, blocking us from the storm above.

No sound. No breeze.

Even the snow hangs motionless atop the trees, as if afraid to fall.

This is where my clever female traps a predator. Her king.

She's chosen a place carved by time like an altar, and the air itself thrums with magical energy. What she didn't account for, though, was her alpha giving in to the rut. Or maybe she did.

Not that it matters either way...

"I found my precious little moon."

SIX
Isabella

·······))) ● (((·······

The instant I hear his voice, every thought stills.

I found my precious little moon.

It's part reverence, part threat, and I cannot control the shiver that runs down my spine at the gutturally spoken words. Low and rough—threaded with something darker that I cannot name but yearn for all the same. Our mating has always been powerful, but as I stand here and watch him take me in, it feels different somehow. New. Hunger, unlike anything we've shared in the past, presses against my chest until my knees nearly buckle.

Instead, I step forward, the cloak moving with each step, exposing more of my nakedness to the man who knows me inside and out. He's seen me at my worst and my best, but the eyes following my movements are full of a desperation I can't name—it's hotter, hungrier, stripped of every ounce of restraint he's ever held.

He's losing himself to the rut.

He's had them in the past; they're as common as a female's heat, but my wolf has always held on to his control. Even at his most

41

fevered, the look in his eyes remained soft and loving. His touch was dominating, yet careful not to hurt me.

The naked man standing across from me, though, this one wants to make me bleed.

And more damning, I want him to.

To break. To claim. To make me take his knot and breed his mate.

"My alpha," I croon, my tone coy, and his head tilts to the side. His lips curve up in a dangerous grin, knot swelling as his shaft thickens further and the angry tip glistens, causing my mouth to water. Then, there's the fur across his half-shifted form while black-tipped claws glint in the filtering light. I'm not sure if it's the moonlight or the aurora shining through, but in its glow, he's beautiful.

A beast. An animal.

King Xadiel Evergreen is magnificent and terrifying, yet I'm aroused. The apex of my thighs is wet and swollen, my skin flushed and slick with need. He's the cause and effect: my mate's nostrils flare, and he takes two steps forward, pausing when a branch above breaks. A tiny one, and the culprit is scared.

A small marten falls, landing near my mate before scurrying away in fright.

Neither of us speaks. No one moves. Our eyes maintain contact, though, deep penetrative stares that say what words fail to at the moment.

I love you.

I live for you.

Catch me.

The latter comes from me, and I take off into the trees before Xadiel can react. It's not lost on me that I've broken a sacred rule: never turn your back on a predator. But I do, and the answering roar that Alpha Evergreen lets loose is delicious. Loud. Full of dominance.

It demands I drop to all fours and spread wide, but I won't make it easy on him.

"Enough," Xadiel grits out, the garbled sound more wolf than human, and I ignore it just the same. I head deeper into the ravine, following a trail of rocks near a stream that leads to near complete darkness. Very little light streams through, but my vision is sharp enough to detect objects near me.

That is, until I hear him.

Feet pounding the ground. His chest purring in a new cadence, yet the underlying edge is clear. Submit. Obey. Come. And while all three sound wonderful, tonight my mate will need to earn the right.

Pushing harder, I undo the clasp of my cloak and let it fall behind me. It's cold, yet the rush of adrenaline and his nearness keep me from feeling the full depth of winter's bite. Instead, I feel warmer the closer he gets, and just as he skims a claw down my right asscheek, the cut deep enough to sting, I turn right where a cave sits empty.

It's large and spacious, perfect for tonight, and I'd had help cleaning it out.

A week ago, while Xadiel was on a short trip to North Dakota, helping an expanding pack, I asked my brother and his fae mate for some help. We cleared out the enclosed space. Stocked it with firewood and food—furs atop a thick mattress with plenty of pillows to satiate my nesting needs.

The place is my gift to him, and in return, I expect to be worshipped the way his ancestors once loved their mates. Untamed. Savagely. Without modern restraints or proprietary notions.

I want to be fucked. I want to be bred.

Loved so thoroughly and deeply that it feels like the first time all over again.

"Last chance, female. Come to me."

"No," I call over my shoulder. We're almost there, but I made a mistake, taking my eyes off the prize. He's closer than I expect, only two steps behind me, and I stumble a bit. Not enough to fall, but the second wasted righting myself lands me in his grasp. "Oh shit!"

"Gotcha." I'm tossed in the air, a scream ripping from my throat before Xadiel catches me. His fur is soft and so warm against my bare flesh, his chest vibrating with a purr that promises retribution. At seven feet tall, he stands proud and hard—every sinuous muscle flexing for me in a show of strength.

Black irises look down at me, the small ring of gold a reminder of his human side, but even that disappears when his nose twitches, head snapping toward the cave entrance. His steps are large and imposing, eating up the space quickly before he pushes open the thick, velvet curtain aside. It's in the same shade of green as our pack's crest.

Through our bond, I sense his confusion, but the moment we step over the threshold, it all changes. Once inside, the golden glow of a well-stoked fire greets us. The chimney was built to lead the smoke out the other side of the cave, invisible to anyone on this side of the dwelling. Its glow is warm and inviting, while a large mattress sits at the center of the room atop a plush rug.

There's a cooler with food. Plenty of fabrics and pelts to keep us warm. A small stream runs along the left wall for fresh water...

His scent and mine are intertwined, creating a comforting perfume that soothes his beast and my witch. *Us.*

"Goddess, Isabella." His black eyes turn molten honey for a second, soft and full of love. "What a special little treasure you are."

"You like?"

"I have no words for how much this means to me," he says. The deep timbre of his voice runs through me, and goosebumps rise across my sensitive skin. It's a tone I know: love and wonder tangled with something heavier.

Gratitude. Awe. Pride.

Xadiel looks around slowly, as if memorizing everything inside —from the smallest item to the intimate touches throughout the den. The flicker of firelight paints his features in gold, softening the savage edges. For this small moment, my king isn't the predator, but a man stripped bare by something simple and given with love.

I swallow hard, heat burning behind my eyes. "It's yours. For when the rut takes hold."

This isn't our alpha home, not the polished halls where we rule here or in England. No. These walls belong to something older. Wilder. Without barriers or rules.

His gaze finds mine again, tender and full of need. "A den."

I nod. "A sanctuary. A special place where you never have to hold back."

"You built me a place to lose control." Xadiel takes in a deep breath again, chest expanding as he swallows hard. Furs and stone, the faint sweetness of jasmine threaded through it, while a woodsy note rounds out the scent. "And you made it beautiful."

"I love you, Xadiel."

"You are my heart." Holding me close to his chest, he walks toward the running stream and drops to one knee. He situates me on his raised thigh, grip careful as one arm cradles my back and the other hand washes my feet with reverence. Slowly, he cleans one, then the other, before moving us to the bed.

There, he retakes his place on the floor in front of me, using an old shirt I pilfered from his hamper—it's unwashed and smells of him after a workout. I'd tucked the white piece next to my favorite fuzzy blanket, and now that scent is being dragged over me from my feet to my legs until it's dropped and my thighs are parted.

Large, clawed hands grip my thighs, the tips breaking skin as I'm pulled to the edge. The sting drags a soft whine from me—a sound that pulls at the beast lurking just beneath his surface. And like I yanked his chain; Xadiel answers the call. One heartbeat, he's my loving mate; the next, he's a beast born of hunger and the need to claim.

His wife. His female. *Me.*

"Look at me," he rumbles, voice roughened by restraint. His eyes are dark again, no gold this time, and the black staring back at me is all-consuming. *My wolf.* Even on his knees, while I sit on the bed, he towers over me—crowds and overwhelms—but I love it. It makes me feel small and delicate against his much harsher planes. "Every breath you take belongs to me tonight, Little Moon. Every sound."

His timbre drops again, vibrating through me. "I own your pleasure. Your pulse. Your heart."

"I'm yours."

"Forever mine." One of his large hands skims from my thigh to ribcage, his touch almost featherlight, until he grips my hair and yanks my head back. My lips part on a gasp, the sting settling where I'm most sensitive, but that quickly turns into a moan when his lips smash to mine.

This kiss is possessive. Dominant and all-consuming.

My alpha kisses me hard enough to steal the breath from my lungs—demanding my surrender, one that I give willingly. I moan, a keening sound he responds to with a grunt, while those clawed fingers wrap around my red hair—grip tight.

Another pull, the pain mingling with the pleasure of his tongue, a sensation I'm helplessly addicted to. His taste is no different. Purely male. Pure him.

Xadiel tilts my head to his liking; his fangs drag across my kiss-swollen lips. The sharp canines break the skin, and a few drops of blood pool there, but before they fall, he licks each one. His growl at the taste is deep and guttural, like a predator savoring his prey.

Because that's what I am.

At his mercy. Here to serve.

"More," I whimper, leaning in to steal another kiss, when he tsks and pulls back. When his eyes meet mine, I find pride with a hint of amusement in his expression.

He's reveling in my desire for him.

"Tell me, my luna. Tell your male what you need."

Goddess, his voice alone…

"Please, Xadiel." I try to lean in for another kiss, but he shakes his head.

"Tell me." He licks his right fang, his muscles bulging from restraint. "Before I use you like nothing more than a hole for my pleasure. Beg me to please you, my love, instead of breeding you like a whore."

Seven
XADIEL
·· ····•))) ● (((•···· ·

"I 'm your whore. Only yours."

"Fucking hell, Isabella." Her acceptance—the truth in those words—they cause my hips to snap forward. I'm pressed against her slick cunt, body forcing her thighs obscenely apart as I slide the thickest part of my cock through her labia. She's bare and slick, body trembling, and I've barely touched her. But then again, she's always been like this. "Always so fucking responsive."

"Please." Goosebumps rise across her skin, and she shivers while her hips tilt in a silent plea for more. That earns my female another rough kiss. It's hard and fast, full of stinging nips between strokes of my tongue, and over too fast as I drag my sharp incisors down her chin.

Then her neck.

I'm leaning over her, forcing her back to arch and breasts to jut out. *Motherfuck,* she's beautiful. All soft skin and lush curves, my mark on her neck while the tattoo of my wolf adorns her supple thigh. Isabella's red hair tumbles over my closed fist in loose waves while those baby-blue eyes watch me from under long lashes. No man could resist her, and I'm a willing prisoner born to serve her.

And in return, I'm gifted her love. Rewarded by her cunt.

"Perfection." It leaves me on a murmur before I pierce the skin above her collarbone, then her sternum, before my fangs embed deep into her left breast. I'm blessed to feel her emotions through our bond—a shock of pain that turns into the sweetest pleasure, and the proof of it bathes my cock. Through our bond, I feel the shock of pain, but that soon turns into pleasure.

Her slick drips as a small tremor rocks through her.

"Oh, *fuck*," she hisses out, trembling as my length flexes against her. She's pinned in place, while the hand gripping her hair moves to her other breast, claws tugging at the stiff peak. I pinch, pull…smack her tit, and my little moon can only moan out a low *please* I ignore.

Her whine and scent change a little then, both tinged with unsatiated need. That won't do.

Extracting my teeth, I pull the tip into my mouth, alternating between flicks and broad strokes of my tongue—sharp nips that draw little cries from her. Her skin grows flushed, sensitive as I lick a path from one nipple to the other, drawing my fangs across soft flesh before suckling the sanguine drops that rise from the small cuts.

I've always enjoyed the taste of her blood as much as her pussy.

It's her. Her essence.

Little Moon digs her fingers into my hair then, nails scraping over my scalp as she holds me against her. Silently asks that I take more of her breast, and I do. Sucking half her tit into my mouth, I lavish the flesh with licks and deep pulls, hollowing my cheeks as her tight nipple swells to a diamond point against my tongue.

And in this moment, I wish she were still producing milk. It's been a few years, our pup is a toddler now, and I miss feeding from her. I miss seeing her round with my child, her body clinging to mine as she demands more.

Of my cock. Of my spend.

My hips jerk, and pre-come spreads across her mound and down to Isa's entrance, marking her as mine. The need to tattoo myself into her every bloody cell is almost overwhelming, but I welcome the madness. This crazed desire to own every sinful fucking inch of her again and again.

A whine slips from her plump mouth, pulling me back to the present. I'm entrapped by the slow roll of her hips beneath me. "I want another pup, Alpha. Breed your female."

Nothing could break an alpha like those words. The small amount of control I'd regained through her thoughtful gift evaporates, and I'm staring down at her, a snarl curling at my lips.

There are no words. There will be no fucking reprieve.

I release her breast and place a hand over the middle of her chest, take in the way my fingers expand from one side of her chest to the other, and the tips of my claws curve around her side. How small and delicate she is, but the gleam in her eyes only tells me she wants this.

Me. My beast.

Fuck, I love her.

Dropping to my knees, I move both hands to her ankles and, with a sharp tug that rips a yelp from her, I bring her pink slit to an inch from my face. The height doesn't work for me, but I fix that by throwing her legs over my shoulder and lifting her arse from the bed. With one hand, I hold a plump cheek, while the other traces from her navel to clit and back again. Two times, the talon dips in, teasing the bundle of nerves peeking out from its hood before I lick the nail clean.

Jasmines. Decadent. Drugging.

She's sweet and tart, the perfect balance of floral, yet the sweet undertones make my mouth water. Isabella is like honey on my tongue, and I bury my face between her spread thighs before her next intake of breath. And that same fucking inhale, it gets caught in her throat as my fangs glide across sensitive skin, leaving a stinging trail behind. I soothe it with a roll of my tongue from her entrance to clit, laving the swollen little bundle.

"Gods, Xadiel. I—"

"I'm your motherfucking everything, Little Moon." Her cunt is pressed against my mouth, her pulse there the same cadence as her heartbeat. Warm. Wet. Heat. I trace her entrance, then dip the tip of my tongue inside, savoring the sweet slick, preparing her to take my knot.

"Don't stop. Feels so good," she moans, her slim fingers digging into the furs decorating the mattress. Her hips buck—Isa tries and fails to move me to her liking. Instead, I eat her like I bloody want. As my cock jerks and drips pre-come, the tip rubbing against the fitted sheet, I flick my tongue low, dragging over my mate's arsehole.

She clenches, then tries to push against me. "I need more...*shit!*"

Before she's done complaining, I retract my teeth from her inner thigh. It's fast and deep, blood trickling from the imprints of my teeth while Isabella's juices drip.

She's gasping and arching—frustrated—but I ignore it and enjoy my meal. I exhale roughly over her cunt, a rumble building as I take hold of her hips. My claws grip her, keeping her in place as I rub my lips and chin over her swollen, juicy mess.

She's desperate.

I'm obsessed.

"Mine." Voice guttural. Deep and garbled.

"I'm so close, Alpha." My response? I lap her like the starved wolf I am. Sucking and nipping—flicking her clit in fast succession —while my little moon quivers. While sweat beads across her skin and her chest flushes, Isa traps her bottom lip between her teeth and begs through hooded eyes for mercy.

I don't stop. Instead, I growl.

The sound is loud, vibrating through her pussy, and her walls contract. Her holes clench hard, as if searching for my knot, and she screams.

"Oh my Gods!" Pleasure crests, the waves rocking her with trembling limbs, eyes tearing up—

I flip her onto her hands and knees. Immediately, she spreads her legs and lifts her arse high, head on the mattress.

She's breathing hard. Still shaky. Cunt and arse are messy and wet.

Motherfucking good girl.

"My little moon." Kneeling behind her on the bedding, I palm a cheek and lean over her. I'm squeezing and petting the flesh, while my lips kiss the nape of her neck and the small bite marks I've left over the last century.

Small. Big. Deep.

I worship each one before nipping my way down her spine, then back up again. Her red hair is sweaty, a few strands sticking to her side, and I fist the locks and wrap them around my fist a few times.

Then I yank, forcing her head back so I can kiss her. Eyes fevered, her delicate fangs drop as our lips meet. The kiss is full of heat and hunger, the taste of blood feeding into the frenzy, and I slam in.

"Xadiel," Isa whimpers, lurching forward, but my grip on her arsecheek and hair keeps her in place. My pace is frantic, each thrust harder than the last as her walls milk me. They squeeze and flex, tighten to the point it's hard to move, but I fuck her through each contraction. My knot is swollen and throbbing—it pushes against her lips with each forceful piston.

I ride her hard. Not pausing when she comes a second time, the words *please* and *alpha* are her mantra.

Calling me her alpha earns her a smack to the arse between slams. Blood rises to the surface, my handprints turning pink, and a jolt of feral greed hits me like a lightning bolt.

She's mine. Only fucking mine.

My hand leaves her hip, slipping between her spread thighs. I trace my claws from her mound to where my cock is pistoning in and out, before sliding toward one of my favorite love bites. It's on her inner thigh, and every time I touch it, she inhales sharply and her arousal blooms. Today, though, I want to play and tease and own every erogenous zone.

"What are you...*oh sweet Goddess*." I don't know if my mate is begging for relief or demanding I don't stop, but she takes what I give her. With my cock buried to just above the bulge at the base, I push the knot against her opening, but don't lock us together. Instead, I use her wetness to tease the crease of her inner thighs where she's sensitive before tapping my mark there.

The bite mark is slightly raised, a little darker than her skin tone, and always makes her shiver. Sensitive, it makes her thrash as I rub across the patch of flesh and extend my clawed thumb to her clit. The stimulation of both—my cock buried deep and knot pulsing—pulls another orgasm from her.

"Such a good little witch for her mate." Pleasure crests, and she squirts, her slick flooding my cock and knot, dripping beneath us to the pelts and sheets. Isa falls forward, but I yank her back to me. "Now give me one more."

"Too sensitive," she whines, legs trying to close, but that's unacceptable. With my knees, I widen her legs to the point she'd be flat on the bed if my hand wasn't splayed across her lower abdomen. I palm the area with my fingers soaked in her come, and pull out so just the tip sits at her entrance. Then I turn her face to mine, black eyes on hooded blue.

I don't say anything while I let go of her hair, run my fingers from her neck to her mouth, and tap her lips. They part, and she immediately wraps her tongue around two digits. Sucking them in, she lets me push them to the back of her throat before I move them to her arsehole.

"I need your knot, my alpha. Give it to me," the last word is a scream, ripped from her throat as I bury myself to the hilt in one smooth stroke. My knot is locked inside her, swollen and stretching her wide while the two spit-soaked fingers massage her arsehole. While I rock my hips, fighting back my orgasm—every nerve ending in my body is alight with pleasure—I slip the two digits to the first knuckle and back out again. While she tightens and mewls, body falling flat on the mattress, I feel the bulge of my cock straining her belly with each short thrust.

From the soles of my feet to my heavy balls, fire licks at my flesh. All I feel and see is her:

Her holes stretched around me.

My fingers are sliding in and out of her arse now.

The satiated grin on her face when she looks at me from over her shoulder.

However, it's the way she says, *"Come for me, love,"* that makes me lose all control.

I'm unable to hold back, locked in with the head of my cock against her cervix. The tightness—the pride coming through our bond—feels like a pulse stroking my knot inside of her...

I come. Rope after rope of my spend fills her and overflows, and through each one, I never stop rocking into her. Never stop pumping my fingers in her arse, and she comes again a minute after me.

Worshipped. Claimed. Loved.

"I love you, Xadiel. You three mean the world to me." Isabella's soft voice is threaded with devotion, and in the haze of rut, I don't question her. Instead, I shift us, settling her over me so her weight is on my chest, my hands holding her steady as I slide in and out of her lazily. My swollen knot keeps us locked, my cock occasionally pumping more come into her womb.

For now, I give her stillness, though. A moment to try and catch her breath.

Because it won't last. Never does between us.

I could spend days like this—wrapped in her scent and magic—and still crave more. My little moon is wonder made flesh, the owner of my heart and soul.

My queen. My home.

Precious One

VI

THE LOVERS

EIGHT
Anaya

·······))) ● (((·······

My phone buzzes before dawn.

Just one vibration, the kind a seer uses when she doesn't want my mate to know she's contacting me. Isabella made me promise her tone stays silent with the single buzz as her marker. She's a sneaky one. To me, at least.

While everyone thinks of her as the responsible one—the glue in the family—I see her true form. My sister-in-law is a spirited witch with a halo of gold and streaks of chaos. She does things her way. Unapologetically her.

Turning my head toward Leo's pillow, I find it empty just as the shower starts in the bathroom. He's up earlier than normal, heading toward the training fields today to run drills with his general. That leaves me with just a few hours to get everything for tonight set in motion, which means if Isabella is texting this early, she saw something.

As I finish that thought, I receive another short buzz.

> Tonight is All Hallows' Eve ~ Isa

> The night when mates remember the hunger that bound them. ~Isa

I smile into my pillow. Of course, she knows I wasn't planning anything *innocent*.

> Is this a warning to abort all plans or...? Anaya

Three dots appear as I hear my mate hum an old tune, singing a line or two here and there.

> Take the obsidian rune. Let him feel the absence and burn for you. ~Isa

A pleasant shiver rolls down my spine then. Part mischief, part anticipation—he's going to be furious in the most delicious way. *Maybe I'll earn myself a spanking...*

> Oh, and hide his favorite shirt. That one is a personal favor. 😈 ~Isa

Giggles slip from me, and I have to bite the pillow to smother them. She always did know how to light a fuse and walk away. Leonardo loves that old, threadbare thing with your *brain on drugs and frying an egg* motif. It's *vintage,* according to him, but to everyone else, that thing is hideous.

I just haven't had the heart to tell him so.

> Done. But you're encouraging bad behavior, Mrs. Evergreen. ~Anaya

Her response comes in quickly and in short text form. Three of them.

> I'm encouraging devotion. ~Isa

> And honoring new blood. ~Isa

> Beneath the next full moon, let him hunt you. ~Isa

New blood? Hunt me?

The latter promises something wickedly fun, while the mention of *new blood* brings a flutter of butterflies to my stomach. I touch the area and find myself smiling. Could she mean…?

> Oh, and wear a short, lavender dress. Something he can tear off when he forgets he's a king… ~Isa

My earlier thoughts are pushed back as the flutter turns into heat. Slow and unfurling, my thighs squeeze tight when I hear the water turn off and the sink start. I can hear him passing the electric razor over his jaw, trimming his low, copper beard. He's gotten even sexier over the last few years, and the facial hair makes me want to bite him.

All the time. Everywhere.

> What exactly do you see? ~Anaya

Because if I'm going to pull this off so I can ride my warlock, I want her blessing. Both his sisters are amazing—have welcomed me with open arms since day one—and I know they'd never leave me out to dry with an angry Wiccan king to deal with.

If anything, they protect me.

Won't deny that getting into trouble with him is pleasurable.

Again, three dots appear. Longer pause this time, but then…

> Stalking. Punishment. Praise. ~Isa

> I will not look deeper; just know you are safe to proceed. ~Isa

Something I would never ask for, but this is her nudging for a little chaos. Blessing our night.

But just to be sure…I triple-check.

> You're really telling me to steal from your brother?
> ~Anaya

> > That's called borrowing, then inviting him to reclaim. ~Isa

Seconds after, another buzz comes in.

> > Run because it thrills you. Because you crave his wrath as much as his worship. ~Isa

The faucet shuts off, and his footsteps shuffle closer; I swiftly put the phone down before snuggling deeper under the covers. I'm excited. My core clenches and wings want to unfurl—stretch, before taking flight, so I can burn off some of this nervous energy—but I slow down my breathing instead.

If Leo realizes I'm awake, he doesn't call me out on it. Maybe because he thinks I'm trying to fall back to sleep. Instead, he walks over to the bed, leans down, presses a kiss to my forehead, and pats my ass twice. My mate heads to the door, sweat towel in his hand, and pauses in the threshold—voice warm and warning.

"Behave, precious one."

The door shuts, and my lips curl into a little smirk.

My king is in for a very big surprise.

Nine
LEONARDO
·····•))) ● (((•·····

The family home shouldn't be this quiet.

Not on this night. Not under a full moon, blessed for the hunt.

Tonight isn't about mortal costumes and candy. For our kind, All Hallows' Eve is instinct and hunger—when bonded mates run free and chase to remember the first claim. One flees, one hunts, and when they meet, the world stands still. It's not a tradition, it's our nature remembering itself.

And may the Gods help anyone who comes between us tonight.

Walking up the stairs, I keep my steps light as I enter our bedroom, but it's empty.

The entire house seems to be.

Soft light glows along the walls, sconces dimmed low while shadows stretch long across polished wood. The air hums. It's charged, a little frantic, and tastes faintly of her.

Fae magic. Wild and sweet and impossible to miss.

My wife. My precious one.

Inhaling deep, I try to find her, but something else is calling to me. Stronger—it yanks me in the opposite direction, back to the first floor and to my office. The sanctum's door is open, and the moment I step through, my head snaps toward the floor-to-ceiling bookcase against the opposite wall.

All of my titles have been turned with the spine facing inward, so all I see are page edges.

Then, there's the wand Gabriella got me as a gag gift a few years ago from some TV-show-based magic shop sitting next to a hand-painted little ghost my mate picked up on the same outing. Both are on the wrong shelf, mixed in with plants instead of mementos I keep among thrillers I like to re-read when I want something entertaining and human.

My half annoyance, half amusement dies when my runes stir beneath my skin—heat rolling, power tingling low in my spine. *Bad little fae.* She touched one of my anchors.

Walking to my desk, I scan the tray holding a total of six runes, one for each pillar of my magic. The obsidian calming stone is missing, the physical pillar that amplifies and steadies the power flowing through my veins. She didn't take from my flesh; Anaya stole the piece that thrums and flows with it.

Those stones are tied to me, to my control. They ground me when emotions rise and anchor my coven when they look to their king to steady the chaos. I use them to help me guide, to calm, to teach—especially young witches who haven't learned how to bend magic to their will.

Fuck, my precious one. This is going to cost you.

She literally took my composure—what cements rationality versus unrestrained emotion.

This was deliberate and methodical. She took advantage of my day out on the field with our army; training took longer than expected, and then my meeting with a coven leader needing assistance went well into the evening.

When the king is away, the naughty fae will plan.

The air stirs, faint fae glamour brushing my senses, her magic stretching against my skin. Something else Anaya's done on purpose. Like a kiss meant to provoke, her message is loud and clear:

Come and find me.

I exhale slowly, a smirk curling at my lips. "Silly girl. I know what you want."

She wants me off-center. She wants the hunt to be real, not symbolic.

Clever, stubborn woman.

I'd had a nice surprise for her tonight, but this changes things.

Turning from my desk, I stretch my neck as the runes along my spine flare, adjusting to the missing calm. Each mark vibrates, as does the physical counterpart on my desk, feeding off each other while my sense of rationality dims to near nonexistence.

I'm not weakened by this, but rather freed.

You made a grave mistake, dear wife.

A big one. A very angry one.

I step into the hallways, head tilted to the side, listening for any sound of life, and find nothing. Silence greets me; no footsteps, no heart, no breaths but mine exist. Something that would be impossible for a coven as loud and full of life as ours, but quiet like this can only mean one thing.

Anaya.

The royal house is always open to our people. Since the fall of Larue and his criminal court, the witches and the fae have lived in peace amongst each other. Two worlds bound by a fragile, hard-fought trust. We have an open passage between the two lands, a give-and-take friendship forged from loss.

Hope blooms where once there was none.

The upstairs is empty and so is the downstairs, but a door near the back is wide open with what looks to be lace crumbled on the ground. It's lavender, my mate's favorite color, and I pick it up as lightning cracks in the distance. In my hands, I hold a pair of worn underwear, her scent on the gusset fresh as is the spot of her arousal right over where the cleft of her pussy touched the fabric.

Delicate and tiny and meant to tease.

She's leading me. Guiding me.

I answer the call through our bond, sending a pulse of desire to her, but curling around that hunger, there's ire. More so when she doesn't answer me. Pocketing her panties, I gaze around the back gardens, a glow of faint silver under the moon. The pathway is lit by solar fairy lights, the light breeze making them appear like lazy, drifting fireflies.

Past the garden, and her scent deepens…

Strawberries and cream. My favorite dessert.

Then wings, distant but distinct. A feather-light giggle riding the wind.

My pulse pounds, and the wards along the familial property hum as I pass them into the woods. I catch sight of blonde hair and violet eyes staring at me from behind a cluster of trees, but I blink and it's gone.

An illusion. Yet her laugh doesn't disappear; it lingers.

It carries through the breeze, then swirls around me, tugging at the invisible bond that keeps us connected. I stop walking and shrug off my shirt, fold it once, and drop it on a chair that absolutely should not be sitting in the middle of the forest.

She's playing.

Not hiding, but unafraid.

Another flicker—her silhouette in lavender, dancing beneath the dark sky. She's wearing a short dress in the same shade of purple as the panties inside my pocket, and I growl her name low as her hands skim down her sides and to the hemline. Anaya seductively sways her hips, knowing exactly what she's doing to me.

My mate lifts the fabric higher with each slow roll of her hips until bare pussy lips come into view.

I've been blessed by the Gods. My eyes catch every sinuous

curve and the wetness shining on her inner thighs—I take a step closer, but she disappears again. I shake my head to clear it, the humor slipping away as my need grows and cock jerks behind the zipper of my jeans.

The taut skin digs into the metal teeth as my side of the bond is yanked, pulling me in her direction. I don't know where she is or how far she's gone, but I can feel her close. Amused and proud of herself.

That sets off the second wave of agitation. My blood heats up at her glee-like edge.

She's outright daring me. Not in trouble, much less afraid of the consequences, but she's going to be when I find her. I wander deeper into the forest and away from the absolute silence of our home. I'm not far from our land's edge—

A hard thump in my chest stops me cold as her much-earned, humor-laced punishment turns into heated anger.

From playful to *I need to find her* before I burn everything around me to a crisp.

Queen Anaya Moore has crossed our royal borders into wild territory.

The wards announced it, and the pain in my chest blooms the farther she moves from their protection. Rogues of every kind travel through the unclaimed territory, from wolves to vampires and the sworn enemies of her people. They roam free here; no laws exist outside of surviving by any means necessary.

"I'm going to turn that pretty little ass red, my precious one. You will learn this lesson." In less than two seconds, I soar from a simmering anger to a red-hot, blood-boiling fury. My walk turns into the pounding of my feet, tearing through the forest until I reach the area of borderland where her scent burns the strongest.

My precious little fae walked through here.

Left me a gift, too.

A few steps from the ward line, a ribbon lies on the grass—

lavender silk tied in that familiar teasing bow. The one she uses when she pretends she can control me. Top, when we both know she's a sassy bottom with a penchant I indulge. Sometimes it's braided into her hair, and others, it's circling her waist like a belt, but the underlying motive is there.

A challenge.

Now, it's lying here wild and waiting for me. Abandoned intentionally, and I pick it up, wrapping the strand around my right wrist before I tear off into a run again. My vision clouds around the edges the more distance I put between us and my lands, and I push harder.

My speed increases with each thump of my heart. Each second apart, I switch between fear for her safety and visions of how I will punish my little fae.

I don't slow down or stop.

Not until a small cabin covered in vines appears.

Firelight dances from the window. I catch movement inside and tear the door clean off its hinges before sending it flying somewhere behind me. A gasp hits my ears; I'm greeted by her wide, doe eyes and plump lips curving into a smile.

That drops the second I stomp toward her, grabbing her wrists and holding her arms out wide before twisting her around. I survey her perfect skin. No mark. Not so much as a scratch.

When I turn Anaya to face me again, my expression is hard. "What the fuck possessed you to leave our lands? You could've been hurt—"

"I wanted to play." No shame, but she does grimace a little.

"You wanted to play?" It comes out as a growl, low and jagged. I slam her back into the wall, pinning her wrists above her head. My hand clamps around her jaw a second before my mouth crashes to hers, swallowing her gasp. That perfect little moan breaks out anyway, sweet and sinful, and my cock strains against my pants.

Her taste on my tongue makes my dick jerk, the swollen head dripping pre-come into the thin fabric.

She attempts to follow my lips when I pull back. "Leo, kiss me. I need your mouth—"

I tsk, quickly leaning down just enough to bite her bottom lip before kissing the tip of her nose. "I played your game, Aya. Now you'll play mine."

Ten
LEONARDO

With her arms still pinned, I skim my free hand down the front of the dress, teasing her erect nipples. They're beaded tight—straining against the thin fabric—and I yank the bodice low enough they slip out.

Perky. More than a handful.

Her nipples are a sweet, rosy pink that makes my mouth water, but I ignore them—a betrayal that earns me a hiss from my wife. Her small fangs peek out from behind a plump mouth, flashing in displeasure.

My response? I smack each tit twice, catching the tips—a warning—before moving further down.

The dress she's wearing has risen, showing off her creamy thighs.

Her pussy is almost on display.

Just a little. Swollen lips are soaked, a few drops of her wetness dripping onto the refinished wooden floors.

Spoiled and impatient.

From the outside, the cabin is average, with vines and wildflowers growing around the property. The inside, though, has an open floor plan and modern amenities. No living room or bedrooms, the large four-poster bed sits against the opposite wall where I have her pinned. No other furniture exists, but there's a fridge and what could be considered a kitchenette with a bathroom to the back as an add-on, and it's small.

The place reminds me of a yurt, without the curved walls.

"You're not being very nice to me," Aya says, voice petulant, back arched in offering.

"Should I be, little thief?" From the corner of my eye, I notice a paddle on the bed and bite back a smirk. *My precious one enjoys a spanking.* "You owe me."

"I have no idea what you're talking about." The tail end of that is said through a whimper as my fingers drift low again, past her chest, abdomen, until I slip between her thighs. I growl as I'm met with bare, soft, and soaked skin.

Fuck, I love her.

"What were you waiting for, hmm?" I pull my hand back, then slap it against her exposed cunt. A small scream rips from her, and I do it again, making sure her clit takes the brunt of it.

Anaya's legs shake, her wings spreading out—a full body shudder rocking her while a stuttered moan leaves her lips. The next hit lands harder, my magic unleashing a sharp electrical shock that leaves her unsteady.

My hold on her arms keeps her up, but the rest of her is pliant and flushed. *Perfection.*

"Leo, I need you." That low, sultry moan with my name on her lips causes my cock to twitch and my hips to flex, looking for the friction I deny myself.

Deny her.

She wants to play this game, test my dominance, and I'll give it to her, but on my terms. I'm in charge.

The anger still pulses despite our proximity and her docility. That rune she *took* calls to me, sensing its owner, and I pause mid-slap. Like a beacon, it flares, but the magic isn't as strong…

My fingers grip her dress, and with one hard tug, I rip it. The first tear is from the hem to her right hip, diagonally, before another yank sends it somewhere behind me. The next piece comes from the bodice, its small buttons pinging all around us, while the top parts reveal nothing but naked, flushed skin and a belly chain. The latter has little blue and purple glass beads, but I'm drawn to the second strand. That one stops right over her mound.

Pushing aside the remnants of her dress, I watch them fall from her shoulders and land around her feet.

Gorgeous. Luscious. Thief.

The rune calls to me again, my skin throbbing with recognition, and I let go of her pinned wrist. "Do not move a fucking inch."

"My king, I—"

Her words are cut off by a quick, yet brutal kiss. It leaves her gasping, my bite to her top then bottom lip a little painful. Her second warning.

"Don't move." With the tip of two fingers, I follow the trail until I find the first of two prizes. Just above her clit, the chain stops, and hanging from the end is my rune.

I tap it once, and its connection to me reignites, thrumming with life, and Aya trembles. Tries to shift away.

I don't allow it.

Instead, I shove two fingers inside her fast and hard—she comes. The first of the night, her hands falling from the wall to grip my arm, trying to shy away, but I only push them in deeper.

"Please, please…oh, Gods, *please!*" Her back arches, pushing her beautiful tits toward my face as a cry leaves her. I'm relentless, pounding her tight hole while using the palm of my hand to rub her clit.

The rune's vibrations help keep her on the edge where pleasure meets pain, overstimulated, but my mate never tells me to stop.

Instead, she tilts her hips and spreads a little wider, chasing another orgasm.

And when she tenses, I pull out.

Anaya whines, her thighs shaking—trying to close and rub together—but I step back, and her weakened legs can't hold her up anymore. Her knees meet the floor at my feet, her eyes staring up at me with undisguised wanton hunger.

My breaths come out in hard pants. Those perfectly parted lips taunt me.

I fist her blonde hair and pull her against my pant-covered length. Rub her mouth across the thick outline a few times before forcing her face up to mine. Then I tie the ribbon around her neck; a cute little bow now hangs at the elegant curve. "You never leave our lands without telling me or the guards, my precious one. You will never put yourself in danger again. Nod if you understand." She does, and I grin down at her. It's salacious and unapologetic against her pout as I tap her nose before wrapping her hair around my fist once more. "Did you want to come again? Were you close?"

"Yes." A meek whisper, but the way she licks her lips is wicked.

"Good. Now pull me out." With shaky hands, Anaya lowers the zipper. My grip on her head never falters as my cock springs free and the tip smacks her nose and lips. *Motherfuck, what a beautiful sight.* More so as her end of the bond sizzles with excitement and yearning, not a single ounce of fear.

"Now what, Husband?"

Thief and cheater; she knows what calling me *that* does to me.

"Open." I tap her mouth with the angry head, rubbing my pre-come across her lips as if it were lip gloss. They're shiny and plump, so soft, but then her warm breath grazes the tip, and I can't help but thrust forward.

The pleasure enveloping my cock as I slide in and kiss the back of her throat is both heaven and hell. Two sides of the same coin, and I'd kill to protect them. This. Her. How she trusts me—knows she's safe to explore and let go—while giving in to a side of her that brings her peace.

She both needs and yearns for my dominance.

"Fucking hell, precious one. Just like that…swallow." Aya does as told, paying special attention to the underside with each thrust of my hips. I stroke in and out, pushing deeper with each pump, and when she slips a hand between her thighs, I pull out, leaving a string of saliva connecting us. "Get on the bed. On all fours."

"Just let me—" The smack of my length against her cheek is loud, and the heat in her violet eyes turns molten. Her wings disappear.

"Now." My mate doesn't stand, but rather crawls to the mattress and climbs up, facing me. Her knees are spread, ass high in the air, and I reward her. Fisting my cock, I leave it a hair's breadth from her mouth. "Go on. Bite it."

Fangs appear a second before the pain, but that quickly becomes pleasure. It feels so good, more so when an electrical pulse shocks me right where my mating mark sits. She's licking now, from tip to mark and then the base, her tongue worshipping my length with alternating broad strokes of her tongue and quick flicks.

I let her do this for a few minutes before reaching over and grabbing the paddle. "Suck my cock, Aya. Show me that my bad little fae is really a good girl."

"Leo, I—"

I slide in deep to the base, my pelvis stopping against her lips. "You're going to keep me right there, use your tongue and swallow. If you try to pull back, it will be worse."

Something unintelligible leaves her, but then she screams. The strike of the paddle leaves a red welt behind in the shape of a carved pumpkin. Pink turns red as it blooms, and I do it again. Three times, pausing when her fangs break skin and she suckles the blood. Her cheeks hollow, trying to pull more of the sanguine drops while the scent of her arousal turns sweeter.

But through the assault, she keeps me in her throat. Works me with the muscles there, and I reward her with two more alternating spanks: one to the area where ass meets thigh, the second between her parted thighs, barely catching her labia.

Her body thrashes, shaking and dripping all over our bedding.

"More?" I ask, pulling my cock halfway out before sliding in, then out again. "Tap my thigh for yes, wiggle your foot for no." She digs her nails into my thigh in response, body languid—relaxed in her position. There are small traces of blood on my shaft from where she cut me; nothing large, and I like the mess it creates.

Sanguine drops across her sharp teeth.

Chin dripping with drool and pre-come.

Face flushed and eyes glazed as they gaze up at me with love.

My wife. My heart.

The last strike comes in fast and hard on the back of her thigh, close to the crease, and her body tenses. For a few seconds, she doesn't move, but then it unfurls. Her pelvic muscles contract, and the orgasm slams into her, causing her eyes to roll back.

Then I fuck her face with complete abandon. The sounds she makes are the perfect soundtrack to our All Hallows' Eve celebration, from whimpers to a glug and the occasional gag when I thrust in too hard.

Grip tight on her hair, I keep her in place while the rest of her shakes, and I pump in and out at a rapid pace. I use her, take my pleasure with deep strokes that cause her to choke on a scream before pulling out, flipping her around, and slamming into her pulsing cunt to the hilt.

Anaya is so fucking tight in her orgasm that the contractions almost push me out, but I thrust through them. This isn't soft or sweet. I ride her with sharp punches of my cock against her cervix while my mouth takes her in a desperate kiss.

Its teeth and tongue, breaths mingling as I grip a thigh in each hand and wrap them around my waist. "Fuck, Anaya. You're my heaven."

I love you, too. Always and forever.

"We are one." With the rune trapped between us, I roll my hips against hers. It's magic vibrates, lashing across my cock while squelching noises fill the room. The sound is obscene yet beautiful, and I close my eyes for a second to enjoy it. My dick drives deep, and her back arches, but I pin her in place beneath me and fuck her through the wave of pleasure.

She's close. So am I.

"Come for me, my heart. Milk my cock." Slipping a hand between us, I stroke the tip of my thumb across her unhooded clit. And fuck me, she clenches so hard—the third orgasm of the night ruins her as she squirts all over us. We're a mess, and I feel more magic than man, the blood in my veins throbbing as I pulse against her stretched walls.

But what breaks me is the feel of my cock bulging against my hand as I slam in deep a final time.

"Yes, Leo. *Oh, Gods*, I feel you," she sobs, hips trying to buck beneath me, and every subtle movement pulls another thick rope of come from me. I fill her to the brim, overflowing in our combined mess, and it's a beautiful feeling to be loved by this glorious woman.

We stay like that for a while, tangled in the sheets with her half-lying on my chest as I stroke my fingers through her damp hair. The world feels quiet. Right. At peace.

"These are the moments I live for," I murmur, voice low. "I could never live without you."

Her lips brush my chest, soft and sure. "Good. Because you never will."

I hold her close after. No more words needed.

Just mine. Just us.

Always.

Minutes pass, and just when I think she's asleep, Anaya whispers, "Do you like the cabin? I bought it from an old rogue couple Isa knows…"

That's as far as she gets.

Next comes the tiniest snore, and I don't have the heart to wake her.

Epilogue

Three days later, beneath a gentler moon, the world breathes
again.

No more warning. No trembling pulse of danger or the
craving for blood.

Only hearth light, warmth, and the soft hum of magic lingering
like smoke in the air.

At the werewolf king's home in England, the night settles with
the presence of family.

Outside, the children play—all cousins—laugh unburdened.
They're free to be wild and explore, while the gods seal their future.
A path already claimed.

They chase fireflies and shadows with the fearlessness only a
sacred bloodline can give.

Inside, the men gather.

A warlock.

A wolf.

A vampire.

Ancient power wrapped in flesh and mortal ease, each holding a glass as the world bends to please them. Their wants. Their needs. Their queens. Two drink scotch, while the latter has dark blood, gleaming ruby-rich inside a crystal glass.

They exude a quiet rumble of pride beneath their casual words.

They've claimed and kept. Hunger sealed into devotion, beast into bond.

Then the air shifts. Soft footsteps. All three women in sync, steady, and excited—the moment they cross the threshold...

Conversation dies mid-sentence, and every head snaps toward them, instincts slamming awake. Their possession is no longer primal, yet no less absolute. This is reverent. Honest and pure. Male eyes track curves and power, hunger softened by the devotion they've earned through battle and blood.

Muscles tense. Throats tighten.

For a breath, the world narrows to the three queens stepping into their dominion.

They're not prey, but the true masters. The reasons why these monsters kneel and kingdoms tremble. Magic glows beneath their skin—ancient, fertile...*chosen.*

Moreover, their mates feel it before they see it.

The pulse of new life, quiet and undeniable. Another generation forms on a single breath.

A gift created beneath the next full moon and born to the three Wiccan royals...

The End...Or is it?
My lips are sealed for now...

Turn the page for a sneak peek at
Siren's Kiss & Feral Beasts

ONE KISS WILL DOOM HIM.
ONE BITE WILL CALM HER STORM.

SIREN'S KISS & FERAL BEASTS

ELENA M. REYES

KAI

"The captain always goes down with the ship."

She drags her sharp, luminescent nails down the front of my trousers, shredding the fabric and zipper just enough to free my cock. It springs free, and I'm throbbing; the engorged head's dripping pre-come while her nose skims me from the slit down to my heavy knot.

There, she pauses and breathes me in.

Her soft lips are a gift, while the bite of her nails on my skin—her full-body shivers—causes my wolf to growl in approval. Nerissa's scent deepens at that, at how close my beast is to the surface, and the natural sweetness of her slick takes on a sharper note as it surrounds us.

A little earthier. More decadent.

My body throbs with need, yet I remain still as both sides of me take in her every movement. My wolf is proud of his treacherous mate, and I find her actions amusing. Adorable.

How she stole from me and then ran is our primal dance.

How she tied me to the ship's mast is foreplay.

"I'm famished, my wolf," my mate croons, looking up at me from beneath her long, dark lashes. Her violet eyes are hooded while her small, yet sharp fangs bite into her bottom lip. "Will you feed me?"

"You're playing a dangerous game, little treasure."

"You don't scare me, Alpha."

"I live to protect you, Nerissa Del Mare. I'd never harm you."

"Then give me what I need, Alpha Daire." Her lips brush across the tip of my cock. The act is reverent and sweet, while the heat in her violet eyes promises a painful reckoning. One soft kiss. One whispered vow. "Feed my selfish desire and need, Wolf. What I'm begging for."

The last word hasn't fully left her sinful mouth before Nerissa flicks her tongue across the engorged head, paying extra attention to the slit where drops of pre-come bead for her. Her hum at my taste is like an electrical shock to my knot—I throb and swell in her tiny hand while she tightens her grip. Those delicate fingers don't meet around my girth. Her mouth stretching over the head looks obscene, but then nothing else registers.

Slow. Wet. Merciless.

Velvet-soft lips wrap around me, working me deeper in small, yet quick bobs of her head until I kiss the back of her throat. Then, there's the scrape of her sharp nails digging into my thighs—the bite of pain is driving my wolf mad, and it's taking every ounce of self-control I possess not to fuck her throat.

To not tear off these pathetic shackles and take control.

I'm allowing my mate this one moment of victory before hunting and mounting my prey. It's in a wolf's biology to toy with its food before tearing into its flesh, and I plan to indulge this beautiful siren until it's my turn to *bite*.

Chains rattle above me, my muscles trembling from the absolute savagery building inside as Nerissa's perfect mouth sucks me. She can't take the full length, but we have the rest of our lives to fix that. To train her to take my knot there, too.

"More," she moans around my girth, her eyes fluttering closed as she savors my taste. The vibrations feel so fucking good, and my chest rumbles with approval while she hollows her cheeks. The look on her face is pure bliss, as if she were praying for mercy and repentance simultaneously—I smile.

There is no escaping my wrath when this is all said and done. *She'll pay for this with her cunt, right before I take her ass. Fair trade after stealing from me.* Because we both know how easily I could snap both these chains and her neck, although I'd never hurt her.

Never her. Anyone but her.

A small string of drool runs down the corner of her mouth and chin, marking the scales still exposed across her collarbone. I grunt at the sight. At the blood there, too. My blood. The deep gouges her nails made on my flesh have dirtied her, and it only serves to heighten her beauty.

Filthy. Sinful. Perfection.

"When this is over, I'm going to give you the world, my female." A promise. My vow. But then the ship groans beneath us; a deafening crack forms a few feet from where she's sucking my cock. We're sinking, and fast—the shouts from my crew break through the raging storm. They call my name, beg me to get off the ship and get to safety, but I don't move.

I'd never ruin her fun. And my female is enjoying herself while ignoring the damage she's created.

The obscene sound of her gagging on my length is worth my ruined ship ten times over.

"Motherfuck," I hiss out from between clenched teeth as her throat spasms, tightly stroking my cock with each swallow. One of my clawed hands embeds itself into what's left of the mast while the other uses the limited mobility the shackle gives me to wrap her hair around my fist.

Grip tight, I keep her in place but don't thrust my hips. Instead, I enjoy the quick bob of her throat on each swallow and the bite of her *nails* as they once again pierce my flesh. The more the vessel tips, flooding each floor, the more aggressive—desperate—my little storm becomes.

The ship tilts further, and a few crates smash against each other. They shatter upon impact, fragments scattering—banging on everything in their path—and yet my mate never stops taking me in deep.

When a small piece of glass from a now broken window slices across my abdomen, I feel her shiver as the air becomes tinged with my blood and need. Her mouth works me harder, deep strokes, before pulling back and licking a path from tip to knot and then to the cut on my stomach.

Both man and beast snarl at her.

Chest heaving. Canines flashing. Drops of pre-come falling to the floor…

The little nymph only smirks at me. "Behave, Wolf."

That's it. Just the directive to stay compliant while Nerissa gazes at the already healing small wound. She follows the movement of each drop and then completely shatters me by licking each one clean. Her tongue is so fucking soft as it slides across the cut, but it's the tingling sensation left behind that causes a hard shiver to rush through me. It's almost volatile; my muscles clench and unclench while my knot swells to near painful.

Her scales, beautiful in their varying shades, also begin to vibrate. The movement is subtle, and the pulse is rhythmic in a pattern of three and four counts between short pauses—I'm entranced. It's a language I don't understand yet, but that I plan to become a scholar of.

"That's my beautiful treasure. Such a good little female worshipping her mate."

At my praise, Nerissa flashes me a sweet look before taking me back into her hot little mouth. Each bob of her head is fast while one hand skims fingers across my knot and lower, squeezing my heavy balls hard enough to sting, but the bite of pain and pleasure only makes me harder.

My release is so close. She can tell, too, and gives the heavy sack a sharp tug.

I release my grip on her hair as water laps at our feet and then our shins. Everything feels in slow motion; the wet heat of her mouth distracts me from the ship's destruction and the worry of my pack members on longboats somewhere nearby. There's not a single fuck in me about the waves crashing and forcing us into what feels like a whirlpool, or the way lightning strikes the wreckage as it drifts out.

All I see and acknowledge is her.

My female. My mate.

Nerissa transforms slowly, her tail shimmering beneath the water, now reaching my knees. What's left of the mast groans, and I do too as she flicks the end back and forth, staying right where I need her.

"Mine."

"I'm yours, Nerissa. Take what you need."

"Never forget that, Alpha," she says, and this time, when she sucks me in, Nerissa doesn't stop until reaching my knot. There, she tightens her lips and teases the underside with the tip of her tongue…

"Fuck," I hiss out from between clenched teeth as the first rope of my spend lands on her tongue. She hums in appreciation at that, hollowing her cheeks and bobbing—milking every last drop. And sexier than anything this gorgeous siren has done…?

The blush on her face as she looks up at me with those violet eyes and swallows.

Perfection. Home. Mine.

Pulling back, she kisses the tip a final time and rises to lay a tiny nip to my bottom lip. Her small fangs cut the skin, her cherry lips now stained with my blood and come as a sharp snap rends the air.

That sound is—

Goddess, everything comes back into focus as I take in a full breath. The late-night sky is lit up with the storm, and rain begins to pelt hard just as the water reaches my chest. The weight of the broken mast is dragging me down, dark water surrounding me, and yet I see it all.

The flash of pain on her face as she slips beneath the water.

The gleam of metal around my wrist.

The light coming from something just past the isolated storm...

And then it's all black. Endless black, until a lithe form swims past me and small fingers skim across my skin. It's a shock to my senses and my beast—the electrical tethers of our bond and the bite of pain as she rips the Cordis Lux from around my neck. My wolf is present in my glowing eyes, taking in the way her clan swims away —they surround their princess—but her movements aren't as fluid.

She's fighting every inch of space between us.

It's there in the lackluster sway of her beautiful tail and rigid shoulders. Slow, as if it physically pains her to swim away from me, but just as they move past the wreckage, she turns a final time, and our eyes meet. I'm growling deep, and the vibrations carry through the water to her.

My mate shivers and extends her right hand out toward me, then pulls it back as I snap each shackle off. Now, there's a hint of nervousness in her expression, and in the semi-formed bond, there's a tug of trepidation for my next move.

And to her surprise, there isn't one. Not yet.

For now, I want her to swim away and hide. I want to earn the right to mount my female.

I'm going to disprove every lie they've fed her.

I will conquer the sea—destroy those separating us—leaving no shelter except me.

I am her home. All she'll ever need.

I'm coming for you, my sinful treasure. There's no escaping me.

Read Here

Fate's Bite Series

READ IF YOU LIKE:

POSSESSIVE ALPHAS
DARK PNR ROMANCE
FATED MATES
EXPLICIT SMUT
MORALLY GREY MEN
SOME STALKING
PRIMAL PLAY
VAMPIRES
WEREWOLVES
WITCHES
FAE

SERIES ORDER:

Theodore & Gabriella
LITTLE LIES
LITTLE MATE

Elena M. Reyes is the epitome of a Floridian, and if she could live in her beloved flip-flops, she would.

As a small child, she was always intrigued by all forms of art: whether it was dancing to island rhythms, or painting with any medium she could get her hands on. Her passion for reading over the years has amassed her with hours of pleasure, but it wasn't until she stumbled upon fanfiction that her thirst to write overtook her world.

She's a short and sassy Latina with an adorable pup, a kiddo that keeps her on her toes, and a husband who claims she'll cause him to go bald prematurely. Lol

Email: Reyes139ff@gmail.com

Newsletter Sign-Up:
https://www.elenamreyes.com/

Elena's Marked Girls.
Come join the naughty fun.
Link: https://www.facebook.com/groups/1710869452526025/

tiktok.com/@authorelenamreyes

facebook.com/AuthorElenaMReyes

instagram.com/authorelenamreyes

bookbub.com/profile/elena-m-reyes

pinterest.com/AuthorElenaMReyes

amazon.com/stores/Elena-M.-Reyes/author/B00E3E26X8

ALSO BY ELENA M. REYES

MY SINFUL VALENTINE

SAVAGE KISS

ONE RULE

MAKE YOU MINE

(Marked Series)

Marking Her #1

Marking Him #2

Scars #2.5

Marked #3

(I Saw You)

I Saw You

I Love You #1.5

Teasing Hands Duet

Teasing Hands #1

Taunting Lips #2

SAFE ROMANCE:

Taste Of You

Doctor's Orders

Back To You

STANDALONES:

Siren's Kiss & Feral Beasts

Craving Sugar

Stolen Kisses